The Last Series

HAL HIGDON

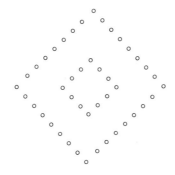

E. P. DUTTON & CO., INC. NEW YORK

For Aunt Irene

LIBRARY OF CONGRESS CATALOGING IN PUBLICATION DATA

Higdon, Hal   The last series.

SUMMARY: A young rookie becomes involved with a group
of fans determined to save the old stadium due to be
demolished at the end of the season.

[1. Baseball—Fiction]   I. Title.
PZ7.H5347Las   [Fic]   74-5023   ISBN 0-525-33395-9

Published simultaneously in Canada by Clarke,
Irwin & Company Limited, Toronto and Vancouver

Designed by Meri Shardin
Printed in the U.S.A.   First Edition
10 9 8 7 6 5 4 3 2 1

Contents

S.O.S.

Ka-Tummm!

Danny Wasocka sat high in the center-field bleachers and heard the mechanical scoreboard thundering behind him.

Ka-Tummm! Every time the pitcher threw, Stratton Field's giant overhead scoreboard recorded the pitch. The numbers were huge, ten feet tall. As the balls and strikes on the batter increased from zero to one to two or three, the scoreboard recorded the count.

The visiting team's pitcher nodded at a signal from his catcher. He wound up, threw. The ball flew toward the plate, curving into the outside corner. *Thwack!* Hoffman, the batter, swung, hitting the ball sharply between the shortstop and third baseman.

This time Danny heard no *Ka-Tummm!* Even if there had been one, the sound would have gone unheard beneath the roar of the crowd.

Nearly twenty-five thousand loyal and noisy fans had appeared at Stratton Field on this sunny Sunday in late September to see their last-place Cobras play the visiting Pirates.

Someday Danny hoped to be playing regularly before those same fans. Maybe soon. Danny Wasocka belonged to the Cobras already. The team had signed him out of college last spring and he had spent the summer playing for one of their minor league teams. At the end of the season most clubs in the majors add younger players to their rosters to test their ability. The Cobras had invited Danny to join them, but because of his minor league team's involvement in championship playoffs, he had arrived late. After today only three more games remained for the Cobras—and for their stadium.

Stratton Field, the old ball park with its exposed steel girders, ancient brickwork, and ivy-covered walls, the last field in the majors without lights for night games, soon would be torn down. Replacing it would be a new $50-million baseball stadium, similar in design to the just-completed football stadium nearby. Next year the fans would be cheering in a new stadium.

Danny leaned forward, excited by the scene around him. At the crack of the bat the bleacher fans had sprung to their feet as though controlled by one mind. Now they remained standing and cheering. Their team, losing 3 to 2 in the ninth inning, had just put the tying run on base.

The noisiest fans seemed to be below Danny, seated just above left field. They wore plastic batting helmets, bright yellow with writing on them, although Danny was too far away to read the words. A pudgy, round-bellied fan now clambered onto the wall above the playing field. Balancing his bulk between field and crowd, he raised a flute to his bulbous lips. To Danny's astonishment, the pudgy fan blew sharply on the flute: *Tweedle-de-deet-de-dee!*

"STRIKE!" responded the crowd.

The flute sounded again.

"STRIKE!"

Danny was puzzled. Why were they shouting "Strike!" Wouldn't "Ball!" be better? At most baseball stadiums they used bugles and the fans shouted, "Charge!" Anyway, Danny marveled at the spirit of these fans, because their team was hopelessly last. The visiting Pirates held second place in the National League's eastern division. Though the season had almost ended, they still had a chance to win the pennant, but the Cobras were going nowhere except home for the winter. Even if they won this game, and the three remaining games of the season, they couldn't improve in the standings. Yet the fans in the bleachers acted as though their Cobras were playing in the World Series.

"STRIKE!" they roared again in answer to the flutist's call.

Perhaps their shouting was some sort of reverse magic to rattle the Pirate pitcher, because he threw wide to Archer, the next batter. *Ka-Tummm!* Then wide again: ball two. The bleacher scoreboard again recorded the count. The fans in the bleachers began stamping their feet and pounding their hands in rhythm.

Clap! Clap! Clap! Clap! Clap!

Danny Wasocka, however, felt another pounding. His stomach. He had rushed to the ball park direct from the airport, arriving in the ninth inning. He had not eaten since breakfast and was hungry. When he saw a hot dog vender pass down the aisle stairs, the pounding in his stomach made him react quickly.

"Hey, hot dog!" shouted Danny.

The vender didn't hear him. "Hot dog! Hey, hot dog!" yelled Danny, but his voice went unheard because of the cheering. The vender continued moving downward. Danny decided to follow him. "Pardon me," he said as he pushed his way toward the aisle.

Ka-Tummm! The scoreboard recorded a third ball. The crowd growled like a tiger ready to pounce. The Pirate catcher walked toward the mound to try to settle his pitcher.

Danny caught the hot dog vender at the moment the batter watched a called strike. In the brief silence that followed, Danny ordered his hot dog. The vender handed him the food and accepted payment while looking over his shoulder at the action on the field. "Where's the mustard?" asked Danny, but his question was lost beneath another cheer from the crowd. Archer had walked, moving Hoffman to second.

As Archer trotted down to first the loudspeaker crackled with an announcement: "The next batter will be Pete Powers!"

"HISSSSSSSSSSS!" sounded the crowd.

Danny was astounded. Pete Powers was the Cobras' best player and also the league's leading hitter. Why was this crowd of seemingly loyal fans hissing him?

The hot dog vender started to move down the aisle. "Where's the mustard?" Danny shouted after him. The vender pointed toward a nearby table. The table had containers for mustard, ketchup, and piccalilli on it—and also one fan who had climbed atop the table for a better view.

"Excuse me," said Danny. "I'd like to get some mustard."

"How can you think of mustard at a time like this?" said the fan, a girl with long dark hair flowing out from beneath her yellow batting helmet. She wore jeans cut short and a bright flower-patterned shirt. "Pete Powers is up," she said, and as though to emphasize her remark went, "HISSSSSSSSSS!"

"How come you're booing Powers?" asked Danny. "I thought he was your best player."

"I'm not booing. I'm hissing."

"Isn't that the same thing?"

"Not in the left-field bleachers," said the girl. "That's the way Vipers cheer—by hissing."

"Vipers?"

"A Viper is a snake, same as a Cobra." The girl pointed at the front of her plastic helmet. Instead of the usual C that the baseball players had on their helmets, hers had the picture of a coiled snake and the name VIPERS.

"I get it," said Danny. "You hiss instead of cheer, and yell 'Strike' instead of 'Charge.' It's not strike as in balls and strikes, but strike like a Cobra strikes."

"Don't bother to show your kindergarten diploma," said the girl. "I believe you graduated."

"Well, I just arrived from out of town," apologized Danny. He held his hot dog beneath the nozzle of the dispenser and splattered mustard on it. "But if you hiss when you're happy, what do you do when you're angry?"

The umpire called a strike on Powers. "BOOOOOO!" roared the crowd.

"Forget I even asked," Danny remarked. He covered his hot dog with ketchup and piccalilli, then sadly shook his head. "That's too bad."

"Now what's wrong?" asked the girl.

"No onions."

She groaned. "You must be a football fan—or something worse."

"What's worse than a football fan?" asked

Danny, taking a bite out of his hot dog.

The girl didn't respond, for the bleachers again exploded with noise. Danny turned toward the field, but those standing blocked his view. He clambered onto the table and saw that the two base runners had advanced to second and third. The Pirates' manager was walking from the dugout to the pitcher's mound.

"Wild pitch?" asked Danny.

"Keep at it," said the girl. "You'll understand this game someday."

Danny noticed that in addition to having VIPERS written on the front of her yellow batting helmet, she had the name LAURA written on the back.

"Hi, Laura," said Danny Wasocka.

"You can read," she replied. "Where's the out-of-town you come from?"

"Wichita."

Laura nodded. "The Cobras have a farm team there."

"Yeah," said Danny. He didn't tell her he played catcher for that same farm club.

On the field the Pirates' manager had motioned for his top relief pitcher, Zeno Gonzorek. As Gonzorek walked in from the bullpen, the people in the bleachers greeted him with a chorus of abuse. "Hey, Gonzorek. We chewed the bubble gum and threw away your picture!" shouted a muscular fan near the mustard table.

He had the name TONGUE on the back of his plastic helmet. The fans nearby cackled happily at his remark.

The person next to him, a slender man wearing glasses, also stood. "Hey, Gonzorek," he cried shrilly, "remember what happened top of the seventh, June 18th, three seasons ago?"

"What happened?" asked the one named Tongue.

"Threw a wild pitch, letting the winning run score," replied his friend, who had SCORECARD SAM on his helmet. The pudgy flutist rose and blew a sour note.

Danny was close enough now to read the name on the flutist's plastic helmet. It said CHARMER. "Charmer?" commented Danny.

"Snake charmer," Laura explained. "He doesn't actually charm snakes for a living. He plays in a symphony orchestra."

"That's a weird cast of characters you have here."

"You're welcome."

"Do you always stand on mustard tables?" asked Danny.

"I'm a nurse. I had to work late today at the hospital. By the time I arrived at the game, all the good seats were gone."

"What's your full name?"

"Laura Addison, but what business is it of yours?"

"Addison? Like in *adder*? That's another snake, isn't it?"

"Ha ha."

"What are the Vipers?"

"You *are* from out of town," said Laura. "The Vipers are the greatest baseball fans in the world. Want a button?"

She reached into the pocket of her jeans and produced a button several inches wide. It was yellow, the same color as her hard hat, and was lettered S.O.S.

"Thanks," said Danny.

"You owe me a dollar."

"A dollar?"

The new Pirate pitcher finished his warm-up throws. Pete Powers stepped up to the plate again. His pin-striped baseball uniform fit him so tightly that it seemed to have been tailored to each muscle. As he waved his bat slowly across the plate, those muscles rippled like a sail in the wind. Even his jutting jaw seemed to have more muscles than those of any other player on the field.

The pitcher stood on the mound, arms at his side. The catcher signaled him with two fingers beneath his mitt. The umpire leaned forward. In the front row of the bleachers, Charmer blew again on his flute *Tweedle-de-deet-de-dee!*

"STRIKE!"

Danny fingered the button he had been

handed. "A dollar is a lot of money for a button that says only s.o.s. That's almost thirty-four cents a letter."

"Thirty cents a letter and a dime for the three periods," the girl corrected him. "Listen, if you can afford to buy a hot dog, you can afford to buy a button. It's for the cause."

"How does your button look with mustard on it?"

"Smashing."

"Well, if it's for the cause." Danny pinned the button onto his shirt and reached for his wallet. At that moment there came a loud *crack*, the sound of a ball being struck sharply by a bat. The crowd roared. Danny turned and saw a baseball flying deep toward him. With two outs, the base runners sprinted toward the plate. The left fielder turned his back on the ball and ran full speed toward the outfield wall until he disappeared from Danny's sight.

The roar of the crowd rose with the flight of the ball, then suddenly stopped—telling Danny that the ball had been caught. The left fielder came running back into view holding the baseball high over his head, the third out. He waved it at the bleacher crowd as though to defy them. But most of them didn't see. They had turned away, as one might turn from an ugly accident. They streamed into the aisles, heading for home.

Danny stood staring at the scene on the field, the bright green grass, the rust-red diamond, the ballplayers in gray uniforms pounding each other on the back, the home team in white moving morosely toward the door in the left-field corner that led to their club house. Groundskeepers appeared to remove the bases and cover the field with a canvas. Danny was awed. He stood on the mustard table watching the field empty of players. Then he remembered Laura.

But when he turned, she already had jumped from the table to vanish into the stream of fans heading for the exits. All he had to show for their meeting was a yellow button on his shirt.

Barrel

Pete Powers, who had hit the long drive that had become the game's final out, reached the club house before any of his teammates. Arriving at his locker, he reached for a small black object. It was a battery-powered calculator, a gift from his fan club. Even before sitting down and removing his baseball spikes, he tapped the calculator's keys. The numbers .347952 flashed on the viewing screen. Powers smiled.

Barrel Barnes, manager of the Cobras, moved past Pete's locker on the way to his office. "Two-for-three today, Skipper," Pete informed him.

The manager mumbled something without stopping.

"That moved the old average up to .348," announced Pete.

The manager mumbled again.

Powers started to follow Barnes toward his office. "Skip, that puts me five percentage points ahead in the batting race. This last series against the Cardinals can't affect our team standing, and I thought—"

"You thought you might like to sit it out to assure yourself the batting title," Barnes said bluntly.

"Well, I didn't want to put it that way, but you've got some rookies coming in. You'll want a look at them for next year."

The manager nodded as though in agreement. "We'll talk about it." He bent over the drinking fountain and took a long drink of cold water. Powers moved back toward his locker, flipping the calculator up and down in his hand as though it were a baseball.

He replaced the calculator on the locker shelf. At that moment the door to the club house opened. Two sportswriters, Holzman of the *Times* and Blades of the *Tribune*, headed toward him. "You were robbed on that last drive," said Holzman. "That center fielder stole a hit from you."

"I wouldn't put it that way." Powers sat down on the stool in front of his locker. "Let's say he stole a victory from our team."

"You're hitting near .350 now," Blades commented. "Think that's good enough for the batting title?"

"I never worry about titles. I just go out each day and play."

"Do you think Barrel will keep you out of the last series to protect your batting lead?" asked Holzman.

"Better check with Barrel. I never tell the manager what to do."

Barnes, still at the water fountain, swallowed so hard he nearly choked. He moved quickly into his office and shut the door. The Cobra manager threw his hat down on the bench, began to remove his shirt, and thought about Pete Powers. If Pete had a chance to go four-for-four or have his team win the game, there was no question which choice he would make.

The manager slipped out of his uniform and headed toward the shower. Barrel relaxed as warm water trickled over his back. During fourteen years as a player in the major leagues, Barrel Barnes had survived mainly on hustle. He played third base with total lack of grace. He fielded ground balls with his chest as much as with his glove, but still threw batters out.

He never batted over .300, but could hit behind the runner, advancing him to second base. Though blessed with only average speed, he stole bases. One time, batting against a pitcher with good control, he had fouled off seventeen straight pitches. The pitcher struck Barrel out, but the following inning got knocked out of the box himself. "I was so tired after pitching to that little runt, my arm had nothing left," claimed the pitcher afterwards.

One theory held by Barrel Barnes was that life was filled with winners and losers. Sometimes a baseball player will make only one hit out of ten times at bat, yet that hit will win a ball game. Other players go nine-for-ten, yet fail to produce those game-winning hits. Also, winning and losing had little to do with talent. Some people lose despite great talent; others win without it. Winning more often was related to desire.

Of course, when you find an athlete who couples talent *and* desire, you have a superior player.

Barnes stepped out of the shower, dried himself with a towel, and began to dress. While he was knotting his tie, a knock sounded on the door. "Come in," said Barrel, suspecting it might be Holzman and Blades finished with their interview of Pete Powers. Instead it was Frank Sparkman, manager of the Pirates.

"Tough game for you to lose today, Barrel," said Sparkman.

"Good game for you to win," grumbled Barrel as he continued to straighten his tie.

The visitor said nothing.

Barrel glared at the Pirate manager. He had played two seasons for Sparkman and disliked him. "Get to the point," said Barrel. "You didn't come in here to apologize for beating me."

The Pirate manager nodded in agreement. "You know how important these last three games are to our team," he began.

Barrel Barnes smiled. He had read the other manager's mind correctly. The Cobras would be playing the Cardinals next. The Cardinals held a three-game lead on the Pirates in the standings. If the Cardinals lost their last three games and the Pirates won theirs, the teams would tie for the pennant. All the Cardinals needed was one victory—or one Pirate loss—to knock the Pirates out of the race. Sparkman had visited Barrel to ask him to play extra hard to win.

"You know how important the last series is to us?" snapped Barrel.

"I know."

"The last series means nothing! Even if we win all three games, we can't move up even one place in the standings. I've got one player on top in the batting race and he's asked me to bench him to protect his average. Every other regular has his mind on packing to get out of town, or is thinking about his off-season job. If I set fire to the dugout they might notice it. I have a half-dozen rookies I've brought up from the minors for a tryout. I need to learn whether or not they can help us next year."

The Pirate manager didn't say anything.

Barrel Barnes continued, "Last June your pitcher decked my left fielder with an inside pitch. Fractured wrist. Lost him for four weeks. Next time you're in town one of your base runners slides high into my second baseman to break up a double play. Six stitches. And you expect me to help you win the pennant?"

"I play to win," said the Pirate manager, now red-faced. He turned for the door.

Barrel waited until he had almost reached it, then said, "Frank!" Sparkman paused in the doorway. "I play to win, too," said Barrel Barnes. "But don't count on me to win your pennant for you."

The Pirate manager glared, said nothing, and stalked out the door, failing to close it. Barrel Barnes, still fiddling with his tie, walked through the door and out into the locker room. The reporters, who had been talking to Pete Powers, turned toward Barrel. "Any chance you might keep Pete out of the lineup for the last three games?" asked Holzman of the *Times*.

"No chance."

"Even if it means costing him the batting title?" prodded Blades of the *Tribune*.

"Pete wouldn't want to win the title sitting on the bench," said Barrel, smiling toward his ballplayer. Powers did not smile back, although the reporters failed to notice this. "Besides, even if it doesn't involve us, the pennant race may hinge on our last three games."

"Does this mean you won't take a look at your new rookies?" asked Blades.

"I'll have plenty of time to see them next spring," said Barrel Barnes, moving past the reporters. He had noticed Al Shinn, his pitching coach, talking to several newcomers, one whose face Barrel recognized from a photograph in a file folder. He walked over to say hello.

"Barrel," said the coach, "meet Danny Wasocka."

"Glad to meet you," said Barrel, offering his hand to the newcomer. His mind was rereading the scouting report in the file folder:

Danny Wasocka. Can catch or play outfield. Strong throwing arm. Fast on base paths. Bats left or right. Signed as free agent out of college. Batted .323 for Wichita in his first minor league season.

"Your team made the playoffs. How did you do?"

"We won," said Danny.

Barrel Barnes already knew that. Danny Wasocka had hit two home runs and batted in seven runs in the playoffs. But he was interested that Danny's response to the question had been to tell him what his *team* had done. There are winners and there are losers, thought Barrel Barnes. But one thing worried him about Wasocka's record. He had quit college after two years. Barrel didn't like quitters.

"How come you didn't stay in college?"

"I didn't like the hypocrisy."

"Hypocrisy?"

"All the good athletes at our college got paid

under the table. The rich alumni slipped them money, bought them clothes, loaned them cars. It was against the rules, but everybody did it. And nobody cared. I finally decided that if I was going to get paid it would be on *top* of the table. So I signed a professional contract."

Barrel nodded and turned to the next newcomer. He didn't place the face. "Where did you play ball this season?"

"Mostly at Eddie's Pool Hall," came the response.

Barrel's eyes lit up. "Eddie's Pool Hall. You must be Harrison Goodpasture." The manager recalled the scouting report on Goodpasture, a pitcher who never had played organized baseball before. His folder contained no photograph, no statistics, no detailed comment. Just a note from a scout whom Barrel trusted, saying:

You won't believe what this man does. Try him!

Barrel would try his grandmother if he thought she could win a ball game for him. "Did you play any when you were in high school?" asked the manager.

"Yeah," said Goodpasture. "Played all the time. That's why I wound up at Eddie's Pool Hall."

Barrel laughed, then introduced himself to the other newly arrived players: Dandridge, a first baseman; Elliot, a shortstop; Martinez, an outfielder. Other rookies had joined the team earlier in the week. Maybe from this collection of youngsters he would obtain some men who wanted to win.

Only one thing disturbed Barnes. It was the bright yellow button on Danny Wasocka's shirt. "How come you're wearing one of those buttons?"

Danny looked down on the button which said s.o.s. "This girl in the bleachers sold it to me."

The manager's eyes twinkled. "Well, I'm not going to tell you to stay away from girls. And you won't have time to sit in the bleachers anymore. But you better ask somebody what that button means before wearing it in the club house."

"Yes, sir," said Danny. He started to remove the button.

"We'll see you at the special workout tomorrow morning at 10:00." Barrel began to move back toward his office.

Pete Powers was standing before a mirror, a can of hair spray in one hand. "Hey, Skip," he said. "That workout tomorrow doesn't include the regulars, does it?"

Barrel Barnes stopped and smiled at him. "The hair looks great, Pete. You can have the day off."

3

We *Love* Our Ball Park

"Break!" shouted Barrel Barnes.

Danny Wasocka walked toward the dugout, sat down, and wiped his forehead with the sleeve of his uniform. They had been practicing nearly an hour Monday afternoon—only rookies and reserves. With no game scheduled, the regulars had been given the day off so Barrel could look at the young players he had invited to play out the end of the season with the Cobras.

Danny leaned back on the grass at the edge of the dugout and gazed up into Stratton Field. Only yesterday, when he had first seen the ball park, it had been filled with cheering people. Now only empty seats stared back at him.

Harrison Goodpasture sat down next to Danny. "Counting the house?" he asked.

Danny smiled. "Reminds me of the crowds at some of the minor league games I played this summer."

"Planning to go back?"

"I'd just as soon stay and play here. How about you?"

"I sure don't plan to go back to Eddie's Pool Hall. Oh, no—although that's where I learned to pitch."

"You threw baseballs at Eddie's Pool Hall?"

"No, *pool* balls. We used to fool around pitching pool balls out front while waiting for the next table. Soon, I realized, hey, I'm pretty good. I mean, man, if you can throw a *pool* ball and make it curve, you're not going to have trouble with a baseball. Then one day this dude drives past, sees me throw, signs me to a contract, and here I am."

"You seem confident you'll make the team."

"Confident? Man, I'm scared to death. Still, I've got my curve, a slider, a screwball. Got a good knuckler, but not much of a fastball. Shoooot—at Eddie's we didn't even use mitts. If you tried throwing a pool ball hard you'd break a man's hand. So you threw the ball tricky—and *dazzled* everybody with your brilliance."

Danny couldn't help laughing. "I'll bet when you stepped up to pitch, the brothers all ran into the drugstore to buy sunglasses."

Goodpasture's eyes brightened. "Hey, you're my man. But wait until I show you my best weapon—the switch pitch!"

"The switch pitch? What's a switch pitch?"

"You've heard of a switch batter, haven't you?"

"It's somebody who can bat either right- or left-handed," responded Danny.

"Right!" said Goodpasture. "Now, a switch pitcher is—"

At that moment a rumbling sound came from beneath the grandstand: *Rrrr! Rrr! Rrumble!* "Sounds like they're tearing the stadium down *today.*" Danny stood and peered over the top of the dugout to try and discover the source of the sound.

Rrrr! Rrr! Rrumble!!

Soon the entire team, Barrel Barnes included, was standing and peering. Finally a mob of people burst through one of the entrances into the grandstand. They wore plastic batting helmets and carried posters, some of which had lettered on them the words of the slogan they were chanting:

"SAVE! OUR! STADIUM!!"

Danny recognized several people from his visit to the bleachers the previous day. They were the Vipers and they appeared to be full of venom as they descended menacingly toward the playing field. Danny glanced toward Barrel Barnes, wondering what the reaction of his manager would be. Surprisingly, Barrel had a wide grin on his face. He rocked back and forth in rhythm to the chant.

"SAVE! OUR! STADIUM!!"
"SAVE! OUR! STADIUM!!"

At that instant a uniformed guard appeared and moved, somewhat meekly, toward the Vipers. They had stopped by the side of the dugout. The guard removed his hat and said, "Gosh, folks, I don't know if you people should be here."

The chanting stopped. A slender girl moved in front of the mob. Danny realized it was Laura Addison, the same girl from the bleachers who had sold him the button yesterday. Her eyes flashed angrily. She waved her sign over the guard's head. "Who says we have no right to be here?"

The guard looked warily up at the sign hanging over his head, as though fearing it might descend any minute. "Well, I didn't mean to say you had no rights," he stuttered, "but maybe you're disturbing the players."

"Who says we're disturbing the players?" Laura glared at the guard. She leaned forward until her chin almost touched his chest. The sign remained poised over his head. It said: WE LOVE OUR BALL PARK! LOVE was written in letters two feet high.

Barrel Barnes raised his hands in a gesture of peace. "These people won't disturb us. They're merely good fans."

"That's right," said an older woman who

stepped out of the rear of the group. "We're not troublemakers."

Barrel walked toward the woman and offered his hand. She accepted the hand and pumped it as though trying to draw water from a well.

"How have you been, Mama?" asked the manager.

Danny Wasocka was standing next to Coach Al Shinn. Danny asked him, "Is that really Barrel's mother?"

"No, that's Mama O'Leary," said the coach. "You know the pizzeria across the street from the ball park? She owns it—O'Leary's Pizzeria."

Danny was astounded. "I never heard of Irish pizza before."

Manager Barnes, meanwhile, continued to talk to Mama O'Leary. She explained how their group had marched to City Hall to see the Mayor.

"Did you see him?" asked Barrel.

"He's never in his office," complained Mama O'Leary. "The only one we ever see is this Mr. Birdbrain."

"Birdsong," Laura corrected her. "Napoleon Birdsong. He's the Mayor's assistant."

"Mama spoke right the first time," snorted one of the Vipers, a tall, muscular man.

Danny remembered him from the previous day—the man called Tongue who had shouted louder than anyone else in the bleachers.

"Today the Mayor was laying a cornerstone," Tongue complained. "Last week he was opening an expressway. Tomorrow he'll be feeding lions in the zoo, or some other excuse. What I'd like to know is how this city gets run if that man's never in his office."

"Computers," said another Viper standing at his side. It was Scorecard Sam.

"What?"

"Computers," repeated Scorecard Sam. "You asked how the city gets run—it's by computers. Two Model X-1000 prime-data computers purring along contentedly in the basement of City Hall, Room 134-A, making 473 decisions a minute, paying bills, routing traffic, choosing contractors for new stadiums while the Mayor is out feeding lions. What this city needs is not an election every four years to decide mayors, but an election to decide computers."

"Well, get me down in that basement. I'll pull the plug on those computers," snapped Tongue. "And while I'm at it, I'll pull Birdbrain's plug, too."

"You can't," said a third speaker. It was Charmer.

"Why not?"

"He's battery-operated."

Danny Wasocka, meanwhile, was trying to get Laura's attention. "Hey, thanks for the button."

She glanced at him and her eyes widened. She

was surprised to see him in a baseball uniform. "You still owe me a dollar for that button," she said finally.

"I left my piggy bank in the club house."

"You didn't tell me you were a ballplayer."

"You didn't tell me you were trying to overthrow the city government. Where can I get in touch with you?"

"I want you to know that I never date ballplayers."

"I only want to give you back your dollar. Listen, maybe I won't make the team."

"In that case, get in touch with me," said the girl. She motioned with her hand, and the Vipers began to move for the exit.

"Where?" Danny shouted after her.

"Leave the dollar with Mama O'Leary," said Laura. She disappeared through the exit.

Mama O'Leary paused before leaving. "Hey, Mr. Barnes, you come for pizza tomorrow after the game. Fifty percent discount because you're a good man."

Barrel laughed. "We'll see, Mama."

"And you," said Mama to the guard who had followed the Vipers to the exit. "You're a good man. You come too."

"Fifty percent discount?" asked the guard.

Mama eyed him. "Twenty-five percent," she said. "You're not that good a man."

When the Vipers all had gone, Barrel Barnes

motioned his players back on the field. The groundkeepers began to move a batting cage into place. Coach Shinn handed a baseball to Harrison Goodpasture. "Let's see you pitch batting practice."

Harrison pounded the ball into his glove, tugged the bill of his cap, and strode onto the pitching mound. He gripped the baseball with his right hand. Danny stepped into the batting cage. Harrison rocked once, then floated the ball over the center of the plate. Danny swung beneath the pitch, sending the baseball crashing against the cage over his head.

Harrison pitched again and Danny hit the ball on the ground toward where the rookie shortstop, Steve Elliot, would have converted it into an easy out. But then Danny's swing began to loosen. He hit the next ball sharply over second base for what would have been a single. He connected on the next pitch, which sailed into the left-field bleachers. The next one bounced off the wall in left center. Then another one cleared the wall.

Coach Shinn had been standing on the mound behind Harrison Goodpasture. "Hey," he shouted. "Get that rookie out of there. He's costing us too many baseballs."

"You stop that, Wasocka," winked Goodpasture, "or I'm going to feed you my eight-ball pitch."

"What's an eight-ball pitch?" Danny laughed.

"*Woosh-zip!* That's my eight-ball pitch." Harrison held one finger in the air as if to say, just wait. He rocked and threw with the same slow motion as he had on the other pitches. Danny cocked his bat and started his swing, but in the last instant the ball suddenly dipped and Danny missed completely. He stood there perplexed.

"*Woosh-zip!*" said Harrison. "Now, do you want to see my switch pitch?"

Barrel Barnes, standing near third base, shouted out to the mound, "All right, Goodpasture. This isn't Eddie's Pool Hall. Save that cute stuff for the other teams."

The pitcher nodded, grooved the ball again, and this time Danny drilled another line drive to the outfield. He dropped his bat and ran once around the bases. "Looking good, Wasocka," Barrel told him as he rounded third base. Barrel also was thinking that the pitch Harrison Goodpasture had thrown had looked pretty good, too.

At the end of practice, Danny moved over to talk to Harrison. "Hey, what's with that eight-ball?"

"I apologize. I shouldn't have thrown it. Not in batting practice."

"I didn't mind. What did you put on it?"

Harrison smiled. "Oh, just some ground-up lizard teeth mixed with toad venom."

"You're kidding me."

"I know," said Harrison. "Actually, it's just a common knuckler. The way you throw it—at least at Eddie's Pool Hall—is you put your fingertips right on the eight in the eight-ball."

"Harrison, you're too much," said Danny, shaking his head. "What are you going to think of next?"

"Well, there's the switch pitch." But Harrison decided not to say any more, so they headed for the showers.

The Spies

After Monday's practice, Danny and Harrison left the club house together. They paused on the sidewalk to gaze at the new football stadium. "Let's see what it looks like from the inside," suggested Danny.

"Why should we care what those football dudes are doing?"

"I used to play the game."

"Not me," said Harrison. "A man can't run too well with a cue stick tucked under his arm."

"Let's look anyway," Danny insisted, and they crossed the street.

The football stadium—Stark Field, Home of the Rockets, named after the team's owner and coach—had been completed only two months before. It resembled a mammoth concrete iceberg. Whereas the grandstands of half-century-old Stratton Field were supported by a lattice-work of steel girders, the new football stadium had smooth lines. Brightly colored metal panels added to its decor. The stadium gleamed in the sunshine. "Looks like it's ready to blast off for the moon any minute," commented Harrison. "Whoooooeee!"

The two teammates walked around the outside of the stadium, finding one gate after another locked. "You'd think this place was Fort Knox," grumbled Danny. "If they build the baseball park like this next year, we may need F.B.I. clearance to play."

"We haven't made the team yet," said Harrison.

"Oh, yeah, I forgot."

After they had nearly circled the stadium, Danny suggested they give up. "Looks like I'll have to use my key," said Harrison.

"You've got a key? Why didn't you say so before?"

"Man, you didn't ask." Harrison reached into his pocket and produced a small silver instrument.

"That doesn't look like a key. That looks like a pair of fingernail clippers."

"One man's fingernail clippers is another man's key," said Harrison. "Stand back. I'm going to dazzle you with my sleight-of-hand." He stuck the end of the fingernail clippers into the lock on the fence gate, jiggled it twice, and the lock sprang open.

"How did you do that?" asked Danny.

"You pivot off your back foot, lead with your elbow, and twist your wrist just as you release the lock. Don't ask questions." He pushed open the gate.

The two baseball players walked through the gate and down a tunnel opening onto an oval-shaped bowl dug below street level. At the bottom of the bowl was a green carpet crossed with white stripes, the football playing field. Above were glassed-in rooms, rented by the football management for ten thousand dollars a year. The cushioned seats in the stadium were colored red, gold, and black, the same colors as the uniforms of the Rockets. Harrison patted one of the seats gently with one hand, as though to make sure it wasn't booby-trapped, then sat down. The cushion sighed under his weight. "Pretty good for a disposable stadium," he commented.

"A *what*?" asked Danny.

"A disposable stadium," said Harrison. "When you're finished using it, you throw it away—just like disposable diapers. They rip off the tax-payers for $50 million to build it, and it takes twenty years to pay for. At the end of twenty years, everybody gets out of the way and, *whummmp!* the stadium automatically self-destructs."

"You're putting me on."

Harrison shook his head and crossed his heart with one finger. "All the supports crumble and the stadium collapses in a pile of dust. A dozen bulldozers push the rubble out of the way—along with a few free agents who couldn't make the squad—and a new stadium rises like a phoenix on the ashes of the old one. Only this time it will cost $100 million and last ten years. Progress. Recently they have been digging under the great pyramids of Egypt. You know what they found?"

Danny said he didn't know.

"Goalposts!"

Danny shook his head. "What about Stratton Field? It's been standing for over fifty years. It probably would stand another fifty if the city didn't plan to tear it down."

"People weren't so cool back when they built Stratton Field," said Harrison. "Today you have to design sports stadiums like automobiles and washing machines—so that they wear out. Then you can go back and sell them another one."

"No wonder the Vipers don't want a new park."

"Well, they've got another problem. Stratton Field's replacement probably won't have any bleacher seats where you can come out, sit in the sun, sip a beer, and watch a game for a dollar. Somebody has to pay for the new stadium and it will be the fans, either at the gate or in taxes. The cheapest seats will cost three dollars and you won't feel comfortable sitting in them unless you're wearing a coat, tie, and fifty-dollar alligator-skin shoes. Progress."

"Did you learn all of that at Eddie's Pool Hall?" C820929 CO. SCHOOLS

"Well, you got to do something with your mind while you're standing around waiting to get into the next game."

The two fell silent and watched the football team in practice. The players would huddle, clap hands, move into place, then explode in all directions. *Click-click-click.* Everything went smoothly like some well-oiled machine. Atop a tower stood Stanley Stark, the football team's owner and coach. Using a hand loudspeaker, he barked strange commands at the players: "Pop-trap-forty-three" or "Mike-box-seventy-two." It sounded like some sort of code to Danny, but the players understood and responded.

Finally, practice ended and the team began to jog slowly around the edge of the green carpet. Coach Stark descended from his tower and climbed into an electric cart to head for the lockers. Danny and Harrison rose to go. Suddenly a shrill whistle sounded. The football coach stood in his electric cart, loudspeaker raised to his mouth. *"What are you two doing up there?"* The question echoed through the near-empty stadium.

"Is he talking about us?" Danny asked Harrison.

The loudspeaker echoed again. *"Guards, find out who those two are!"*

Danny looked around and saw uniformed

guards moving toward them from several directions. "I think we've been captured," said Harrison. "Remember, don't admit anything other than your name, rank, and baseball uniform number."

The first guard arrived and confronted them. "All right, who are you guys?"

"Foreign spies," cackled Harrison. "But we've already swallowed our code books."

"Don't kid the man," said Danny, getting worried. He turned to the guard. "We just wandered in to watch practice."

The guard glowered at them. By this time a half dozen other guards arrived. One, who seemed to be in charge, asked, "Who are they?"

"Seem to be just a couple of clowns who wandered in off the street," said the first guard. "I guess we'll have to take them down to the coach's office."

"Aren't you going to inform us of our rights to remain silent before you bust us?" asked Harrison.

"Look, you guys aren't supposed to be in here," said the head guard. "We could lose our jobs. Coach Stark won't even let his mother inside the stadium when his team is practicing."

"We don't want to cause any trouble," said Danny.

"Yeah, we don't want to get the coach's mother mad at us," added Harrison.

The two rookies, accompanied by the head guard, walked back out the tunnel and climbed into a waiting electric cart. "It's your fault, Wasocka," Harrison whispered to Danny. "I never should have let you bring me here."

"*I* brought *you* here?"

"That's what I said. My mama warned me about keeping bad company."

"*Me*, bad company?" said Danny. "What about those fingernail clippers of yours?"

"I've got to keep my fingers trimmed, man, or I can't throw my eight-ball pitch."

"Well, we're both behind it now."

"Behind my fingernail clippers?"

"No, behind the eight-ball."

The guard drove the cart around the rim of the stadium to an elevator. The elevator door opened and the guard drove inside, pushing a button. They descended soundlessly. When they had dropped four levels, the elevator door opened with a hum. The cart rolled into a long concrete corridor with the football dressing room at one end.

"This place reminds me of a bomb shelter," muttered Danny.

"Ain't that the truth," Harrison agreed. "If the atom bomb ever falls, the only survivors will be professional football players."

The cart stopped and the guard ushered Harrison and Danny into an office. A man sat at a desk sorting letters. The guard told him, "Tell Coach Stark these are the two intruders." Then he left.

The man motioned for them to follow him into a second, inner office. This office contained a half dozen plush chairs and sofas, but no desk. The walls were paneled with teak. The carpeting was green, the same color as the football field— only without white stripes. The man left them and they were alone for a minute. Then another door opened and in strode Stanley Stark, owner and head coach of the Rockets.

Coach Stark was built like a bulldog, and the moment his eyes met those of the two intruders, he barked, "What team you spying for?"

Harrison fell suddenly silent. "We play for the Cobras," Danny finally blurted.

"The Cobras," snapped Coach Stark. "You're lying. We don't play any team called Cobras!"

"We're baseball players," explained Danny.

"Baseball players?" asked Coach Stark. "Oh, *those* Cobras. You're from that baseball team next door."

"That's right."

"What the heck you doing over here? I don't come spying on your practices."

Danny Wasocka didn't say anything. He thought that even if the football coach did spy on their practices, he wouldn't learn much except which player was endorsing which bubble gum. "We didn't—" he began to apologize.

"Forget it," said Coach Stark. He pushed a button on the arm of one chair and a door in the paneled wall slid open to reveal a refrigerator. "You guys want something to drink?"

"I'll take a cola," said Harrison. Those were the first words he had uttered since entering the office.

"Same here," said Danny.

"Sorry, all we have is Fizzle-Up," said Coach Stark. "They advertise on our scoreboard. You seen it? We can run instant scoreboard replays of the action right after it happens on the field. Almost as good as staying home and watching the game on T.V."

The coach removed two cans of Fizzle-Up from the refrigerator and handed them to his guests. "I didn't realize you guys were baseball players," he continued. "What are your names?"

"Harrison Goodpasture," said Harrison Goodpasture.

"Danny Wasocka," said Danny Wasocka.

Coach Stark squinted at him. "Wasocka? I've heard that name before. Didn't you used to play quarterback for Western University?"

Danny admitted he had. The coach turned to Goodpasture. "Where did you go to college?"

"U.C.S.L."

"I've heard of U.C.L.A., but never U.C.S.L."

"That's the University of California in St. Louis," said Harrison innocently. "It's a new branch."

Coach Stark stood puzzled for a moment. "They must not have a football team," he said, then went on, "Say, you've got some nutty fans out at your games."

"How's that?" asked Danny.

"Those Vipers. They're fighting the new stadium, but your players will love it. Deep-cushion benches by each locker. Soft lighting. Stereo music in the showers. You'll win twice as many games next year."

Danny had gulped down the Fizzle-Up. "We better get going," he said. Harrison agreed.

"I'll show you a shortcut out," said Coach Stark. He pressed another button, causing a section of teak paneling to slide open. "It's a secret exit I had built. Comes out below the parking lot. I use it to avoid signing autographs. Nobody knows about it."

They moved into a small elevator. The elevator rose. When its door slid open they stepped out into the sunlight—and into a crowd.

Danny, Harrison, and the football coach were surrounded by the fans from the bleachers. Danny quickly spotted Laura, Charmer, Tongue, Scorecard Sam, all those who earlier had been at the baseball practice, and—standing near the rear—Mama O'Leary. He also noticed a T.V. camera.

Coach Stark was so surprised he let the elevator door slide closed behind him. He began to fumble in his pockets for the key that would open it again, but several microphones had been shoved at him. One was held by Brent Moss, sportscaster for a local T.V. station. "Coach Stark," asked Moss, his voice dripping with honey, "what do you think of the fight against the baseball stadium?"

"Well, I'm in favor of it," said Stark, still fumbling for his keys.

"You favor fighting the stadium?"

"No, I favor the stadium," said the coach. "I mean, no comment. No comment!" He found his keys, opened the door, and disappeared back through his secret exit.

The T.V. announcer turned to Danny and Harrison, who remained standing on the outside. "What about you two gentlemen?"

Harrison stuttered, "Well, I dig what the football coach says."

"You mean, you favor the new stadium?"

"No, I dig his 'no comment.' "

"And you, sir?"

The T.V. camera turned to focus on Danny Wasocka. The honey-voiced announcer stuck the microphone under his chin and smiled. But Danny was looking past the microphone and camera into the crowd where he saw Laura wearing her yellow s.o.s. button and holding her sign saying WE LOVE OUR BALL PARK!

Danny said nothing, but reached instead into

his pocket for a bright yellow button the same as that worn by Laura. He pinned the s.o.s. button onto his shirt, and the cheer that rose from the crowd was as though he had hit a grand-slam homer in the fourteenth inning of the seventh game of the World Series.

The honey-voiced announcer turned to face the camera, smiled, and said, "The score at Stark Stadium is two 'no comments' to one 'no stadium.' This is Brent Moss speaking for Channel Two Sports."

5

O'Leary's Pizzeria

While the T.V. crew was putting away the cameras and microphones, Laura turned to Danny. "I guess I never learned your name."

"Danny Wasocka," he replied, "but I thought you didn't date ballplayers."

"I'm not asking you for a date," snapped Laura. "I'm just asking your name."

"Danny Wasocka."

"You told me that. Who's your friend?"

"That's Harrison Goodpasture, but he doesn't sign autographs after 5:00 in the afternoon."

"Pleased to meet you," said Laura. She offered her hand to Harrison.

"Likewise." The pitcher grasped her hand.

"We marched over here to see if we could hassle Coach Stark into a statement," explained the girl. "He's such a pompous man that he comes unglued easily. But we didn't know we'd get an endorsement from one of the Cobras."

"*Future* Cobras," Danny corrected her.

"And maybe not too 'future,' once the Cobra management sees that telecast," worried Harrison.

"Future or not, I still owe you a dollar for that button."

"Forget it," said Laura. "But if you'd like to join us, we're going over to Mama O'Leary's for pizza. You'll have to pay for that."

Several of the marchers already had begun to leave. They walked past the new football stadium and the old baseball park until they came to a small brick building with the sign O'LEARY'S PIZZERIA hanging over its door. "I never did find out why this town had Irish pizza," commented Danny.

"Mama actually comes from Italy," Laura told him. "Her late husband was an American sailor."

They moved inside where another sign identified the pizzeria as HOME OF THE VIPERS. Each noon before a Cobra home game, O'Leary's Pizzeria would fill with fans. They would eat, then drift over to take their bleacher seats, often still holding steaming pieces of pizza in their hands.

The Vipers usually arrived for the game just in time for the last line of the national anthem, which they had amended slightly—

Oh say, does that star-spangled banner yet wave,
O'er the land of the free
And the home of the *Cobras*!

The Vipers thought it unfair that only Atlanta Braves' fans should have their team mentioned in "The Star-Spangled Banner."

Monday being an off-day, there were only a few people in the pizzeria when the marchers arrived following their rally at the stadium. Laura, Danny, and Harrison settled down at a table with several Vipers, including Tongue, Charmer, and Scorecard Sam.

Mama O'Leary donned an apron and walked over to wait on the group. Danny, reading the menu, asked, "What's this Shamrock Pizza?"

Corned beef and cabbage, with mozzarella cheese," explained Mama, "in memory of my late husband."

"That's real soul food," said Harrison. "We'll take a large one."

After Mama had taken the order and left, Charmer placed his flute on the table and sighed. "Another day, another defeat."

"Cobra fans are used to defeat," grumbled Tongue. "That's why we're so tough."

"Too true," sighed Scorecard Sam. "We've gone twenty-three years, eleven months, and eighteen days without winning a pennant. It's hopeless."

"If you feel that way, why do you come out to the ball park?" asked Danny.

"Sometimes I think it's out of sympathy," said Tongue.

"No, I disagree," commented Scorecard Sam.

"Stratton Field is the last home in America of daytime baseball. It has actual grass growing in the infield. A blend of Kentucky bluegrass and Creeping Red Fescue, by the way. But it's real, not plastic grass that must be painted green. Stratton Field has ivy growing on the outfield walls. Not advertisements telling you to buy this smooth-riding car or fly that friendly airline."

"I never attended a baseball game until this year," admitted Laura. "When I came to town to work as a nurse, I rented a second-floor apartment from Mama O'Leary over her pizzeria. I hardly noticed the big building across the street until spring when the crowds appeared."

"Then you became a fan?"

"Not at first. The cheering bothered me, especially when I worked nights and had to sleep days. But later in the summer I got off work at 3:00 in the afternoon, when it was too late to go to the beach. So I started sun-bathing in the top row of the Stratton Field bleachers. By the seventh or eighth inning you can walk through the gates without a ticket. After a while I became interested in those funny people down on the field wearing knickers and oversized gloves. So I moved down with the Vipers."

"And now you like baseball."

"I still don't understand the game. It's just fun to sit in the sunshine with your friends and make noise without somebody complaining that you're disturbing the peace."

"Those days are gone," sneered Tongue. "In the new stadium it probably will be against the law to cheer."

Scorecard Sam agreed. "And you'll have to wear a coat and tie and act like a gentleman."

"So what do you plan to do?" asked Danny.

"Ah, me," said Charmer, dipping into the relish tray with one pudgy hand.

Tongue looked toward Laura. "Just hope that our leader here comes up with a new idea. She's the one who got us organized. We would have sat around and let them tear the seats right out from under us if she hadn't taught us to do something besides boo umpires."

Everybody turned toward the girl. She shrugged. "I suppose I've always been an organizer. When I was in third grade I organized a strike at my school so we could get chocolate milk with our lunch."

"Did you get it?"

"I got a good spanking."

"We're not talking about chocolate milk," rumbled Tongue. "We're talking about a $50-million stadium. And if we don't do something about it soon, we'll have to become roller derby fans for excitement."

"I admit I've run out of ideas," said Laura.

There was a moment's pause while everybody looked at each other until finally Charmer broke the silence. "The game is never over until the last man is out."

"What's that supposed to mean?" snapped Tongue.

"It means," Charmer explained, "that they can't tear down Stratton Field until the season ends. And until that time we can still think of a way to block the new stadium."

"We've been thinking, and marching, and complaining all month," growled Tongue. "Nobody listens. We can't even get through to see the Mayor."

"Birdsong," said Charmer.

"Birdsong?"

"Birdsong," Charmer repeated.

"We're ten runs behind in the ninth," moaned Tongue. "Two outs. Nobody on. And now our weakest hitter steps to the plate singing bird songs." He raised his hands in a gesture of helplessness.

"Wait a minute," Laura interrupted. "Maybe he has got an idea. We can't see the Mayor because his assistant, Napoleon Birdsong, always stands in the way. Now, if we can find out why, we might succeed."

Scorecard Sam was thinking too. "I could take a trip down to City Hall. There might be some information worth uncovering. You never know."

"What are you going to do," Tongue said skeptically, "talk to the computers?"

"That's not such a bad idea either."

"The game is never over until—" Charmer began again.

But someone near the T.V. set shouted for silence. They turned and saw the smiling face of sportscaster Brent Moss filling the screen. "Today the Vipers held a rally to protest the planned $50-million baseball stadium," Moss announced.

The picture shifted to show the rally. The cameras focused on "no comments" by Coach Stark and Harrison Goodpasture before showing Danny Wasocka pinning the S.O.S. button on his shirt. Finally the smiling face of the sportscaster appeared again. "But unless the Mayor decides otherwise, it looks like the Vipers will lose—just like their team, the Cobras, usually lose."

The group at the table groaned and turned away just as Mama O'Leary appeared with two trays of steaming hot pizza. They forgot their problems for a moment and reached for the food in front of them. Except for Charmer. He picked up a slice of pizza, propelled it toward his mouth, and was about to take a bite when he paused and uttered a single name: "Birdsong!"

Hot Dog

"What do we owe the Pirates?" asked Coach Al Shinn. He answered his own question. *"Nothing!"* He was sitting in Barrel Barnes' office talking to the Cobra manager before Tuesday's game.

"What did they ever do for us?" continued Shinn. *"Nothing!* We've got to worry about next year, not about whether some other team wins the pennant."

"And you feel that means playing our rookies?" said Barrel.

"Right."

Barrel Barnes frowned. He sat behind his desk, pencil poised over the starting-lineup sheet. Within the next few minutes he would have to hand it to the umpires, but he had not yet penciled in a single name.

He knew that Coach Shinn had a good point. They could benefit by seeing how some of their young players would react under pressure. Many of his veterans were tired. Pete Powers wanted to protect his average, and it probably would be good for season ticket sales next year if Pete won the league batting title. But Barrel still hesitated.

Another factor was that two of his better rookies—Wasocka and Goodpasture—had been caught by the T.V. cameras yesterday afternoon in the middle of a Viper protest march. Barrel had thought it funny, but the club owner had not. He wouldn't be happy if Wasocka and Goodpasture started today's game.

"We're in last place playing with veterans," argued Coach Shinn. "We can't drop any lower with rookies in the lineup."

Barrel objected. "That's not completely true. This club is coming around. We've improved. We could be contenders next season. All we lack is extra effort, more hustle. The players need to get the feel of winning. They need more confidence. Maybe, by sweeping this last series, they can gain it."

"And maybe—" added Shinn "—by adding a few top young players, we also could become winners. Now is the time to find out if these youngsters can play major league ball."

"True," admitted Barrel Barnes. He knew they had a good crop of rookies. He knew that several might help them next year and the only question was, Which ones? But he also knew that he was going to play his regulars.

Without saying another word to his coach, he

penciled in the names of the same players who had been starting all season: Hoffman at first; Archer at short; Powers in right. On down the list: Harmon, Roddy, Wynder, Murray, Pidcock, with Schroeder pitching. He tore off a copy and handed it to Coach Shinn.

Shinn glanced at the paper, said, "It's your team, Barrel," and left to post the lineup on the club house bulletin board.

Many of the players, including Danny Wasocka, gathered to look at it. Coach Shinn glanced at Danny. "You've got a great future—if you ever decide to become a T.V. weatherman."

Danny turned red. The other ballplayers laughed and whistled. Laughing harder than anybody was Harrison Goodpasture. Shinn turned next to him. "As for you, Goodpasture—"

"Me, Coach?"

"You hang in there with those 'no comments.' " Shinn stalked out the door toward the field.

Ten minutes before the start of the game, Barrel left his office. Only a few players remained in the club house. One foursome was still involved in a bridge game that had continued on airplanes, at hotels, and in locker rooms for six months. Catcher Ralph Pidcock was fastening his shin guards. Pete Powers sat in one corner reading a copy of *Sport* magazine that featured an article on himself.

"Skip, you're not going to lose me that title," said the muscular right fielder. "My wife's building a new kitchen. I need the extra money a batting title will bring."

"No, I'm not going to lose you the batting title," said Barnes, without breaking stride.

"Hey, Skip," Powers shouted after him. "If the Pirates couldn't win the pennant themselves, they don't deserve having us win it for them."

Barrel pretended he didn't hear. Walking toward the plate to give the starting lineup to the umpires, he reflected on a pennant race ten years earlier. His team had come to the end of September only one game out of first, had won their final three games, but remained one game behind because the team the league-leaders were playing had loafed and lost. He didn't want to be accused of doing the same.

But after their game with the league-leading Cardinals had gone only a few innings, it appeared not to make much difference. The manager had started Gary Schroeder, a sixteen-game winner and the ace of his staff. Against the Cardinals he lasted only two innings, giving up six runs. Pete Powers came to bat in the bottom of the third and homered over the right-field wall, making the score 6 to 1. Pete rounded third already looking toward Barrel in the dugout, hoping to be replaced.

The Cardinals scored two more runs in the

fourth. The Cobras got one back in the fifth and another in the seventh. They still trailed 8 to 3 in the eighth inning when Pete Powers came to bat with nobody out. On a two-and-one count, he dribbled an easy grounder down the third-base line.

Pete flung his bat in disgust. He started to trot—not run—toward first. The third baseman easily fielded the ball, stopped as he saw Powers wasn't trying, relaxed, took two steps, and threw over the head of the first baseman. Pete Powers found himself safe on an error. The right fielder, however, retrieved the ball before he could go to second.

Barrel Barnes stood on the edge of the dugout, burning with anger. He turned and the first player his eyes lighted on was Danny Wasocka. "Get in there and run for Powers!" he roared.

When Pete Powers returned to the dugout, Barrel snapped at him. "If you had hustled, you'd have been to second." The big batter frowned and sat down.

The next batter, center fielder Kevin Harmon, strode up to the plate. As Danny stood on first base, he heard the sound of a flute from left field followed by "STRIKE!" Charmer was doing his job. It takes a special brand of fan, thought Danny, to get excited with three games left in the season, his team in last place, and five runs behind in the eighth inning. "STRIKE!" echoed the cry of the Vipers.

Danny turned his attention to the mound. The Cardinal pitcher was intent on his catcher's signals. Danny took two steps off the bag. The pitcher nodded at the sign. Danny took another step. The pitcher barely glanced at him, then threw a fastball. It plopped hard into the catcher's mitt for a strike.

The catcher fired the baseball back to his pitcher. Danny walked back toward the bag, kicked it, then took three steps away from first. The pitcher looked at his catcher. Danny edged another half step closer to second. The pitcher glared at him, looked as though he wanted to throw to first to hold him closer, then seemed to decide not to bother. The batter swung at the next pitch, a slider, hitting it foul.

Danny tried to think like the Cardinal catcher might. They had a two-and-nothing count on the batter. If Danny were catching, he would call for a change-up, high and outside, to try to sucker the batter into going for a bad pitch. Harmon was a left-handed batter. Under this reasoning, the pitch would come across the plate slow and to the catcher's mitt hand, meaning he would have to step left to catch it and thus be in a poor position to throw to second. The pitcher, with a five-run lead, had been ignoring the base runner. Danny thought he could steal second—if he could get a good lead. Four steps off the bag might be enough.

The Cardinal pitcher stretched and Danny

moved down the line two, three, and then four steps. The pitcher remained frozen for a second, looking at the base runner, wondering whether or not to hold him on. Finally he decided that with a five-run lead, it wasn't worth the effort. The pitcher glanced away, and in that instant Danny broke for second base.

The pitch was high and outside, as Danny had predicted. The catcher snatched the ball and made a perfect throw to the covering shortstop. But Danny slid cleanly into the bag before the throw arrived.

The Cardinal shortstop started to laugh. "You want to make sure they notice you in the press box, huh, rookie?"

Danny blushed. Maybe stealing a base wasn't such good strategy. He rose and brushed the dust from his uniform.

The other Cardinal infielders also had smiles on their faces. The third baseman shouted, "Hey, hot dog. You going for third? Let me know, so I can get out of your way."

"Don't laugh at the rookie," responded the second baseman. "That's probably the first stolen base the Cobras have made all year."

Barrel Barnes, standing in the dugout, heard the remark and winced. The Cobras were not a running team. That was one reason why they were in last place. They rarely gambled. They rarely tried for an extra base. If Wasocka had been thrown out stealing with his team five runs behind, Barrel would have been forced to give the rookie a good tongue-lashing for stealing without orders. Since he succeeded, Barrel chose to handle the matter differently. When Danny looked toward the manager to judge his reaction, he saw Barrel looking the other way.

The pitcher threw again. This time Harmon swung and hit under the ball, sending a lazy blooper into short center field. The second baseman and shortstop charged after it, but it dropped just beyond the second baseman's mitt. The center fielder tried for a shoestring catch, and missed.

With nobody covering second, Danny had moved nearly to third. As soon as he saw the ball drop, he started to sprint. The Cardinal center fielder picked up the ball slowly, figuring neither runner would risk advancing another base.

He figured wrong. Danny had flown past third with no plans of stopping. When the center fielder finally saw Danny heading home, he threw quickly. Too quickly. The throw was high and Danny scored. Harmon advanced to second.

The play seemed to bother the pitcher. He walked left fielder Ike Roddy on six pitches, and when third baseman Steve Wynder hit a triple and scored on a bad throw, the Cardinal lead had shrunk to one run. The Cardinal manager waved in a relief pitcher, but two singles and a double later the Cobras had a 9 to 8 lead going into the ninth inning.

Barrel opened the ninth with his best relief pitcher, Bob Lake, who struck out the first batter, then allowed two singles. Barrel sighed and walked to the mound to talk with Lake. Warming up in the bullpen was Don Alger, who had a sore arm, and Harrison Goodpasture.

"How do you feel?" Barrel asked.

"I've got nothing on the ball," admitted Lake. "It's been a long season." Catcher Ralph Pidcock nodded in agreement.

The manager looked out toward the bullpen at Goodpasture. Alger couldn't even knock over a stack of amusement-park milk bottles with his fastball and Goodpasture had never pitched in a game. Not just pitched in the major leagues, but pitched *anywhere*—except back of Eddie's Pool Hall.

"Just try to keep the ball low," instructed Barrel, and walked helplessly off the mound.

The next batter hit the first pitch hard up the middle, but third baseman Wynder stabbed at it with his glove and converted what should have been an extra-base hit into a double play. The Cobras, surprisingly, had won 9 to 8 and, unless the Pirates lost that night, the Cardinals would have to wait at least one more day to clinch the pennant.

Above left field, the Vipers gave one last, mighty cheer as they moved through the exits. Barrel headed toward the club house, Coach Al Shinn at his side. "What do you think?" asked Shinn.

"We burned them with our regulars."

"But it took a rookie hustling on the bases to set the fire."

"True," admitted Barrel Barnes. "Very true."

It's Always "Next Year"

Danny and Harrison stopped at O'Leary's Pizzeria following the Cobra victory and found Laura sitting with Tongue, Charmer, and Scorecard Sam. Only Charmer was eating. He congratulated Danny. "Good base running."

"Thanks."

"That may be the last base they'll let you steal," advised Tongue. "It's part of the standard contract when someone signs with the Cobras. Section XVIII: *Thou Shalt Not Steal Bases.* The Cobras haven't stolen a base in twenty years."

"Twenty-three days," corrected Scorecard Sam, lowering a copy of *The Sporting News.* "On September 3rd, bottom of the fourth, two men out, Dennis Murray stole second base."

"He didn't have to steal second base," argued Tongue. "Murray's a second baseman. He already owns second base."

"The Cobras were batting. At the time *they* owned second base. Murray stole it from them."

Tongue frowned. He turned toward Charmer, who was stuffing a peanut butter and salami sandwich into his mouth. "Did you see Murray steal second base?"

Charmer shrugged. "I must have gone out for popcorn."

"So did the Cobra coaches," snorted Tongue, "or they never would have allowed the steal. It's against the standard contract. Section XVIII."

Danny laughed, but felt obliged to object. "I think you'll see a new team under Barrel Barnes."

Harrison agreed with his teammate. "Right. Wait until next year."

Tongue moaned. "That's the cry of the Cobras: Wait until next year!"

"Cobras don't cry," Scorecard Sam informed him. "They hiss."

"Normal cobras hiss. These Cobras cry—and it's always 'next year.'"

"With the team playing in that new stadium, I'm not sure there will be a 'next year' for me. Who wants to watch baseball from a cushioned seat?"

"Not me," admitted Charmer, finishing the last bite of sandwich. He dusted his fingers on the napkin tucked under his chin. "I'm not sure I'll even fit between the armrests of their new seats. I like benches, the kind we have in the bleachers now. Gives me more room to spread out."

"Listen, with your spread they should make you buy three tickets," said Tongue.

"When you think of how much ticket prices are going up to pay for that $50-million stadium," sniffed Charmer, "I'd still be ahead."

"That's another problem," said Scorecard Sam, turning to Danny. "Have you seen what they've got planned for center field?"

Before Danny could reply, Sam answered his own question. "A water fountain! A million-dollar water fountain with twenty-six spigots, colored lights, and controls so you can play it like an organ. I've examined the plans and they must have been drawn by Dr. Frankenstein. Every time someone on the home team hits a home run, the fountain gushes pink and violet."

"We've got nothing to worry about," Tongue commented. "Nobody on the home team hits a home run. That's Section XIX."

"September 14th, top of the sixth, two men out, nobody on," barked Scorecard Sam.

Tongue glared at him. "You're going to tell me that at that point in time somebody from the Cobras hit a home run."

"Pete Powers."

"That's different. Sub-section B of Section XIX. Pete Powers is allowed to hit home runs because they never win ball games."

"Regardless of your sub-sections," continued Sam, "that fountain is the crowning insult, besides which the Cobras will be the only team in the major league that, in addition to a trainer, will need to hire a lifeguard."

Laura shouted for them to remain silent and pointed to the T.V. set behind them. The group turned and was greeted by the smiling face of sportscaster Brent Moss. "Now for the highlights of today's Cobra game," intoned Moss.

Suddenly Danny was stealing second for the second time today, and on the next play he scored. The telecast showed all the Cobra heroics and ended with the final double play. Moss announced that the Cobra-Cardinal game had been the only one played in the major leagues this afternoon. "All other games will be held under the lights. The Pirates have jumped to a two-run lead in the first inning of their twilight game in New York, meaning they're still in the pennant race."

Then Moss grew serious. The sports scores dispensed with, it was time for news of greater world import. "Some citizens," he began, "have expressed concern about plans for the new baseball stadium. We decided to ask the Mayor, His Honor E. Forrest Wells III, for an opinion on the matter."

The T.V. picture changed to a scene that had been recorded at City Hall earlier in the day. Standing next to Moss was a man wearing a maroon sports jacket and plaid bow tie. He looked from Moss toward the camera and his face exploded into a big grin. Several Vipers started to boo, but Laura hushed them. Brent Moss thrust his microphone under the Mayor's chin, tried to match his smile, and asked, "Mayor Wells, what is your opinion?"

"Golly, Brent," replied Mayor E. Forrest Wells III, "I thought everybody loved baseball."

"The people behind the protest say they love baseball, but don't love the plans for the new stadium," Moss explained.

"Well, Brent, you can't keep everybody happy. You'll always find those who protest no matter what you do. As mayor of this fine city, however, I have to choose what's best for all the people. And—heh, heh—right now that means going through with my promise to the baseball fans of this city that they will have their new stadium before next season begins." The Mayor smiled again at the camera.

Moss turned back to the camera, the shine from his smile and that of the Mayor nearly blinding those watching at O'Leary's Pizzeria. "Mayor Wells' opinion," said the sportscaster, "is that the baseball fans of this city deserve a new stadium. This is Brent Moss speaking for Channel Two Sports."

In O'Leary's Pizzeria, it was as though the visiting pitcher had knocked down one of their heroes. "BOOOOOO!" Someone flipped the switch on the set. Brent Moss' smile faded to a tiny circle of light.

"The nerve of that Mayor," Laura huffed. "He believes he's doing *us* a favor by building a new ball park."

"He probably hasn't even been to a ball game in twenty years," rumbled Tongue.

"Five months and seventeen days," said Scorecard Sam.

"What?"

"The Mayor throws the first ball out at the start of each season."

"I forgot. Then he hires a masseur to treat his sore arm."

"Birdsong," suggested Charmer. "He's the one who keeps His Honor from learning the truth."

"Birdsong or not, we've got to convince the Mayor that we don't want another $50-million instant stadium," Laura insisted.

Mama O'Leary appeared at that moment and plopped several hot pizzas down on the table. Harrison Goodpasture stared at the one in front of him. "What is this?"

"Soul Pizza," Mama said proudly.

"Soul Pizza?"

"Cheese, sausage, and collard greens."

"Mama, you are out-of-sight!"

Danny asked her how she had enjoyed the day's baseball game.

"Oh, I never go to the games," said Mama. "I'm too busy making pizza."

"Then how come you're so interested in saving Stratton Field?" Danny wanted to know.

Mama O'Leary shrugged.

"Very simple," Laura explained. "When the city builds the new stadium they're going to bulldoze this block and turn it into a parking lot. Mama will lose her business—and her home."

Mama O'Leary nodded without saying anything. Harrison Goodpasture's eyes grew wide in horror. "Tear down the only restaurant in town that serves Soul Pizza? That's a disgrace!"

"We think so," said Laura. "That's why we're not going to give up until we've had a chance to explain our case to the Mayor. But we haven't been able to get near him. He won't see us."

"Won't see you?"

"We never get any closer than his assistant."

"Birdsong," Charmer said again.

"A disgraceful man," growled Tongue.

"But we're not giving up until the last man is—"

Laura brought her fist sharply down on the table, halting the conversation. "It's time to quit talking and start planning." She reached into her shoulder bag and produced a folded piece of paper. When she unfolded it on the table, it turned out to be a map of the city's downtown area. "This is City Hall," she began. "It will be called Contact Point A."

See the People

On Wednesday morning Napoleon Birdsong stood on the fourth floor of City Hall outside the Mayor's office and nervously tapped the button on his portable two-way radio. With it, the Mayor's assistant could talk with men scattered outside and inside the building. Birdsong prided himself on how smoothly he planned the Mayor's daily schedule. He succeeded because he used every available modern device to speed His Honor to and from his public duties.

Today, like every Wednesday, was See-the-People Day. "I want to keep in touch with the common folk," Mayor Wells often said. That was the politician in him speaking. He wanted to shake every hand offered him, kiss the cheek of each baby he saw.

Birdsong recoiled at the thought that this ever might happen. He believed that the Mayor must be protected from this instinct of the politician;

otherwise the business of running the city never would get done. Fortunately, Birdsong had mastered the art of moving the Mayor past crowds. The people got to see the Mayor, and the Mayor got to see the people, but never did they quite touch.

On this particular See-the-People Day, Birdsong had scheduled a half dozen visits around the city for Mayor Wells. There was a new subway train to ride, a groundbreaking ceremony, a birthday party for the fire commissioner, and still more. Through the grace of God (not to mention the wisdom of Napoleon Birdsong), His Honor would arrive at each visit precisely on time.

This was no easy task in this day and age. Years ago people visited City Hall seeking jobs or favors. They wanted their garbage collected. They wanted traffic tickets fixed. They wanted summer work for their children planting trees with the park district. Any smart secretary could handle these people by referring them to an alderman. The alderman did the favor and at the next election collected their votes.

But today people visited City Hall in groups of hundreds and thousands, chanting and waving signs. They were not as easy to handle. They weren't interested in jobs or favors. They didn't want to see a secretary. They had no use for the alderman. They wanted the Mayor. They wouldn't go away, but would return day after day, still chanting, still waving signs, still angry that their demands had not been met.

Napoleon Birdsong took delight in protecting the Mayor from such people.

Right now the biggest troublemakers were the Vipers, who opposed plans for the new baseball stadium. Though few in number, they made more noise than any protest group that the Mayor's assistant could remember during seven years at his job. Perhaps it was because of the practice they had in screaming at umpires. Birdsong planned to make certain that this group never got anywhere near Mayor Wells.

Birdsong tapped the button on his portable two-way radio and spoke. "How does it look today?"

A voice crackled in his ear. "Only a few protest groups waiting outside. A bunch of parents wanting control of their schools at the north exit. A black-power group at the east exit. A crowd of people against pollution to the south. The biggest group is at the west exit. They're all wearing baseball helmets and S.O.S. buttons."

"The Vipers," snarled Birdsong. He thought for a moment, balancing the problems posed by each group in his mind. "We'll go south. Have the Mayor's car ready to move toward that exit on signal."

"Yes, sir," crackled the voice in his ear.

At that moment Mayor E. Forrest Wells III appeared in the door of his office. He was rubbing his hands together and smiling, as though the best part of the day were about to begin. He looked eagerly toward his assistant. "Ready to go, Birdsong?"

"Ready, Your Honor," Birdsong replied, then glanced at his watch. The time was exactly noon.

The Mayor strode through the corridor and into the elevator, his entourage trailing him like a flight of ducks. As the elevator moved from the fourth floor toward ground level, Birdsong checked his two-way radio again. "How's it look out there now?"

"Some of the baseball fans have begun to move toward the south exit," announced the voice in his ear.

Birdsong frowned. "Then we'll exit north."

The elevator reached the ground and Birdsong pointed the way toward the north exit. At that moment his two-way radio crackled again. "The baseball fans have started to run toward the north exit."

"Then we'll take the east one." Birdsong put a firm hand on the arm of the Mayor. "We've decided to go out the other way," he said.

"Oh, certainly," said the Mayor, and turned in the corridor. But again the voice sounded from the radio. "Now the baseball fans are running around to the east."

Napoleon Birdsong cursed under his breath.

The baseball fans seemed to be capable of reading their minds. More likely they also had a radio. Oh, the deviousness of these protest groups, thought Birdsong. He would have to start using secret code. He tugged at the Mayor's sleeve again and pointed behind him. This time he didn't announce the change of plans by radio. "I wish you would make up my mind," sighed the Mayor. "I don't want the people to think I'm indecisive." Mayor Wells turned once more, the group with him turning also like players in a game of crack-the-whip.

They finally reached the west exit. Birdsong sighed with relief as he found it unguarded. Then he noticed the single woman in a black shawl seated on the steps. "Mr. Mayor," she began as she rose from her seat.

Birdsong whispered into his two-way radio. "Limousine to west exit—fast!"

The Mayor turned toward Mama O'Leary, his face radiating warmth at the thought of greeting a voter. "Mr. Mayor," Mama O'Leary said again.

Birdsong grew tense and spat into his radio, "I said *fast!* "

Mama O'Leary now had the Mayor's hand and was pumping it. The Mayor pumped back, and for a moment the two stood there pumping and smiling. "Mr. Mayor," Mama O'Leary continued, "I was too tired to run to the other side with the rest, so—"

The Mayor's limousine careened around the

corner and skidded to a halt by the curb.
Birdsong tightened his grip on the Mayor's arm
to urge him toward the car. For a moment Mayor
Wells seemed torn between two duties, but followed his assistant's lead. "It's a pleasure to
meet you, Madam," he said as he slid into the
back seat of the car. "I wish I had more time to
talk now, but if you'll call my office—" The door
shut on the limousine and it roared away, leaving Mama O'Leary standing alone on the curb.

"By the way, what was it she wanted?" the
Mayor asked Birdsong as the car pulled into traffic.

"Whatever it was, we'll handle it," suggested
Birdsong.

"Yes, by all means," said the Mayor. "She reminds me of my own mother, rest her soul."

Meanwhile several dozen members of the
Vipers came running around the corner, too late,
to find the Mayor gone and Mama O'Leary standing alone on the sidewalk.

"Did you get a chance to talk to him?" asked
Laura.

"Well, I said hello," Mama replied. "He looks
like a nice boy, but so busy. My! "

Laura turned to Scorecard Sam, who had a
two-way radio in his hand similar to that carried
by the Mayor's assistant. "Call for the bus," she
instructed him.

Sam spoke a few words into the radio, then

turned back to Laura. "Where do we go now?"

"Contact Point B. The subway. The Mayor is dedicating a new subway train."

"I'm going to stick here and rummage through the City Hall records to see what I can find," suggested Sam. Charmer came chugging around the corner, puffing hard from the effort. Scorecard Sam handed him the two-way radio.

"What am I supposed to do with this?" asked Charmer. "I'm not a radio operator. I'm a musician."

"Then listen carefully. You might hear some bird songs."

As Scorecard Sam disappeared into City Hall, a school bus painted bright yellow with the slogan SAVE OUR STADIUM on the side halted at the curb. The Vipers quickly boarded. In less than a minute they had driven off on the trail of the Mayor.

Mayor Wells and his party, meanwhile, arrived at the subway entrance and met a crowd of officials. An escalator whisked them underground. At the subway platform, a gleaming new train awaited them, its door open, only a yellow ribbon blocking passage.

The Mayor walked up to the ribbon, then hesitated. "What's this, wet paint?"

"No, you're supposed to cut the ribbon," Birdsong whispered.

"There seems to be some sort of writing on it."

The Mayor bent down and began to read.

BUILD SUBWAYS NOT STADIUMS, said the writing on the ribbon.

The Mayor looked puzzled. Birdsong turned red. He looked over his shoulder at a city official. "Quick, the scissors."

The city official turned to a subway official behind him. "Quick, the scissors."

The subway official poked the man behind him. "Quick, the scissors." He thought the man to be a subway worker, since he was wearing a yellow hard hat.

"The scissors," said the man, who was wearing a batting helmet, not a hard hat. It was Tongue, and he handed an object to the subway official.

"The scissors," said the city official, handing the object to Napoleon Birdsong.

"The scissors," said Birdsong, handing the object to the Mayor. Then to Birdsong's horror he suddenly realized he had just handed His Honor a switchblade knife.

Flick! The Mayor pressed the button on the handle of the switchblade, but instead of a gleaming blade, out popped a yellow rose. Startled, the Mayor dropped the switchblade-flower onto the platform and backed through the door of the subway train. The ribbon parted. The crowd cheered. Photographers snapped pictures.

Birdsong motioned to two policemen standing nearby and directed them to Tongue. "Arrest that man!"

The policemen clapped their arms around him. "What's the charge?" asked Tongue.

"Carrying a concealed weapon," said Birdsong.

"Weapon?" protested Tongue. "That was no weapon." But Birdsong had stepped through the subway door. It closed behind him. The train moved off down the track.

On the street above, Charmer sat in the bus, radio in hand, and relayed information to the waiting Vipers. "They've just arrested Tongue for carrying a concealed flower."

Laura nodded her head. "We expected that. Move out to Contact Point H."

"What about Contact Points, C, D, E, F, and G?"

"We have people there already."

And down below, the train carrying the Mayor rattled through the subway tunnel. As they came to the next station the train slowed slightly, but did not stop. Mayor Wells glanced out the window and was surprised to see a group of people wearing yellow batting helmets standing on the platform. They held a banner saying:

HERE WE ARE

"What was that?" said the Mayor as the train continued past the station.

"What was what?" asked Birdsong. He had been looking at his schedule and had not seen the people on the platform.

"There were some people with a banner saying, 'here we are.' Where are they, anyway?"

"Behind us, I hope," mumbled Birdsong. But
as the train continued down the track they came
to a second station, a second group of people,
and a second banner:

IN THE DARK

"It's some sort of continuing message," decided the Mayor, "like roadside advertising.
'Here we are, in the dark. . . .' "

They passed the third station and banner:

ASKING YOU

And at the fourth station, they read:

TO SAVE OUR PARK

Finally, at the fifth platform, the waiting people tipped their helmets. Their banner said:

THE VIPERS

"I just don't understand what's going on
today," said the Mayor, "but that was sort of
cute." There were no more banners and the subway train moved up an incline, out of the tunnel,
and onto the middle of an expressway. Automobiles rushed by on both sides. Mayor Wells
asked his assistant about their next stop.

"The end of the line," said Birdsong.

The Mayor wrinkled his nose. "Isn't that the
garbage dump?"

Birdsong smiled. "Well, it *was* the garbage dump, or rather a *landfill*, to use a pleasanter name. But now the city plans to build a new low-cost housing development there."

"Oh, yes," said the Mayor. "I remember now."

"We're due in ten minutes for the ground-breaking ceremony." Birdsong glanced at his watch and was relieved to see they would arrive on time.

"A groundbreaking ceremony? At the garbage dump?"

"Please," smiled Birdsong. "Refer to it as Parkway Gardens. That's the new name." But as he spoke, his smile faded, because out the window of the train and on the nearest lane of the expressway he had spotted a yellow bus with SAVE OUR STADIUM written on its side. The bus picked up speed until it was moving along the expessway at the same speed as the Mayor's train.

"What's wrong now?" asked the Mayor.

"Nothing," said Birdsong, and turned to point the other way. "Say, isn't that an interesting-looking sausage factory on our left?"

The Mayor glanced the other way for a moment, but suddenly a voice echoed across the expressway, louder than even the sound of the train or the traffic. "Mr. Mayor," boomed the voice.

The Mayor turned and saw the yellow bus traveling beside them. The voice was being amplified by a loudspeaker atop the bus. Sitting in the front, microphone in hand, was a woman in a black shawl. "My goodness," said Mayor Wells. "Isn't that the same woman who spoke to me at City Hall?"

Birdsong scowled and barked into his two-way radio, "Give me the police. This is the Mayor's party. We're being trailed by a strange-looking yellow bus on the expressway near 35th Street. We want the bus halted and its occupants arrested."

The voice of Mama O'Leary, meanwhile, continued to blare through the loudspeaker. "Oh my," said the Mayor. "That woman really must have something important to say."

Napoleon Birdsong was furious. "She's a crackpot. They're all crackpots. Where are the police?"

"This is Squad Car 703," came a voice over the radio. "Uh, we're heading south on the expressway to intercept yellow bus."

On the bus, Charmer grinned at the two-way radio in his hand. "Hey, this is neat," he said. "You can pick up police calls. I wonder if I can get the baseball game. It should be starting about now."

"Give me that radio," snapped Laura, grabbing it out of his hand. She pushed down the button and began to speak. "Car 703, this is the Mayor's party again. Disregard last message. Yellow bus turned off expressway at 63rd Street."

"Roger, Mayor's party. This is, uh, Car 703 disregarding message."

Napoleon angrily shook his radio. "This is sabotage. Somebody else is on this wavelength. Someone else is—" Birdsong halted and looked out the window at the yellow bus pacing their subway train. Laura was sitting by the window holding a two-way radio identical to his. The girl smiled, waved, and blew him a kiss. "Aha!" said Birdsong.

"Mayor's party, did you just say aha?"

"No," said Laura.

"Yes!" roared Birdsong. "Arrest that yellow bus!"

"Uh, roger, Mayor's party. We'll resume pursuit of yellow bus."

"At last," sighed Birdsong.

"Mr. Mayor," Mama boomed. "About that baseball stadium. I have a pizza parlor—"

At that point the train with the Mayor on it plunged into a dark tunnel that curved to the left and under the other lane of the expressway. It headed off in the direction of the garbage dump. Mayor Wells gazed out the window into the darkness. "I guess they're gone," he said. "My, I like pizza as much as anybody, but that's a strange way to advertise it." Napoleon Birdsong sank backwards into his seat and mopped his brow.

Meanwhile, on the bus, Laura groaned. "We've lost them," she said as the expressway turned right toward the southwestern suburbs.

"He looked like such a nice boy," sighed Mama O'Leary. "Too bad I didn't have time to talk to him."

Laura, almost in tears, handed the radio back to Charmer. "There must be some way to get that man's attention."

Charmer looked at the radio in his hand. "I wonder how the Cobras are doing?" He jiggled the radio. "Hey, does anybody know the score?"

The bus carrying the Vipers hadn't gone more than a half mile from where the tracks and highway divided when a police car, its blue light flashing, siren whining, pulled them over to the side of the road. A police officer climbed out of one of the squad cars and stuck his nose in the bus door. "The Cobras are losing two to zip in the second," he growled. "But that's nothing compared to the score against you."

Goodpasture's a Southpaw

Krak! The ball flew off the bat and over the head of Wynder, the third baseman. It curved toward the foul line, hit the grass only inches fair, and bounced into the Cobra bullpen in left field. Danny Wasocka, sitting in the bullpen, jumped out of the way so as not to interfere with the play. The ball struck the grandstand wall and caromed back onto the field. By the time Roddy, the left fielder, had picked it up and thrown it to the shortstop, base runners stood on second and third and another run had crossed the plate. The Cardinals led the Cobras 3 to 0 in the fifth inning.

Danny settled again in his chair, tipping it against the grandstand wall. As he did, the phone connecting the dugout with the bullpen rang. Coach Al Shinn picked it up and heard the voice of Barrel Barnes. "Give me the big left hander." Shinn put down the phone and pointed at Clarence Bernard, a lanky left-handed relief pitcher. "Warm up," he said.

Bernard shrugged off his jacket and stepped onto the bullpen mound, which was crowded between the left-field line and the grandstand. He began lobbing the ball easily to Collins, the second-string catcher. Barrel Barnes walked from the dugout to talk with Nash, his starting pitcher, but didn't take him out. By the time he had returned to the dugout, Bernard already had begun to throw hard.

The next two pitches by Nash were balls. The phone rang again. Coach Shinn answered it and relayed the manager's message: "Goodpasture, he wants you throwing, too."

Nash got the next pitch over the corner of the plate for a called strike. Harrison grabbed a baseball with his left hand and moved next to Bernard on the bullpen mound. Danny rose to catch his teammate's warm-up throws. Nash's next two pitches, meanwhile, were balls, and the batter walked.

"That hurt," Danny commented over his shoulder to Coach Shinn.

"Barrel probably told Nash to throw wide," said Shinn. "If the batter goes for a pitch, he probably won't hit it. If he walks, it sets up a possible double play. The next batter doesn't hit as well and is left-handed. Barrel can use a left-handed relief pitcher against him and pick up an edge. Smart baseball, that's all."

Barrel Barnes moved out of the dugout again and waved his left hand. Bernard took one last throw, picked up his jacket to place over his left shoulder, and began to walk slowly toward the mound. Once there, he took five more warm-up throws, nodded his readiness to the umpire, and threw a single pitch. The batter hit it on the ground to the shortstop. Archer to Murray to Hoffman for a double play, and the Cobras were out of the inning with no more runs scoring. Shinn told Harrison to stop throwing. They returned to their seats.

Almost immediately a piece of paper attached to a string dropped from above to dangle in front of Danny's face. Often fans would lower programs or autograph books with pens attached to have players sign them. But this paper had no pen attached. Danny reached for one he had in his jacket pocket.

"Don't sign it, man," warned Harrison.

"Why not?" asked Danny. "It's my first big-league autograph."

"Coach says you sign nothing during the game. Sign one now and the fans will be dangling by their toes trying to get you to autograph their foreheads."

Danny looked upward and shrugged. Then he realized that the fan holding the other end of the string was wearing a batting helmet, a Viper. Danny wondered why he was in the left-field grandstand instead of the bleachers. "I don't want an autograph!" Scorecard Sam shouted.

"What?"

"Read the message!"

Danny looked at the piece of paper again and saw writing on one side. "The fuzz busted the Vipers," said the message.

Danny turned toward Harrison. "Hey, according to this note, the police arrested Mama O'Leary and the Vipers."

Harrison shook his head. "Those poor dudes will never get to talk to the Mayor."

Danny was about to ask Scorecard Sam for more information when there was a loud crack of wood meeting leather. The few fans who had appeared for the Wednesday game roared their approval as the ball hit by Harmon, the center fielder, settled into the right-field bleachers. The Cardinals now led the Cobras only 3 to 1.

Danny stood and watched Harmon trotting slowly around the bases before turning back to the grandstand. But Scorecard Sam was being led away by one of the ushers. Danny decided that anything he could do would have to wait until after the game.

In the next inning, Bernard retired the Cardinals in order, but Pidcock, the catcher, walked in the Cobra half of the sixth. Barrel lifted Bernard for a pinch hitter. Goodpasture was told again to warm up along with Don Alger, a former twenty-game winner now past his prime. The pinch hit-

ter struck out, ending the inning, and Alger went
into the game.

In two more innings Alger allowed four hits,
but no runs. Goodpasture was up and down in
the bullpen in both innings. The Cobras scored
another run in the seventh on Archer's home run
and two in the eighth on four straight singles,
one of them by Alger, who was attempting to sacrifice. The Cobras now led 4 to 3.

The first batter to face Alger in the ninth lined
out to Harmon in center and the second singled.
Barrel Barnes yanked his pitcher. Tom Dudas, a
left hander who had been warming up with Harrison, was called in. The next batter hit a sharp
grounder between first and second. Murray dove,
knocked the ball down, and threw out the batter,
but the runner moved into scoring position on
second.

On the mound, Dudas looked worried. He
wiped his forehead and threw the first pitch to
the next batter into the dirt. Pidcock had to dive
to save it. The next pitch also was a ball. Barrel
Barnes was on the phone to the bullpen. "If he
loses this man it brings up Gonzales," said Barrel, mentioning a Cardinal left-handed batter.
"I'm going to want a right-handed pitcher.
How's the bullpen look?"

"A few more pitching changes and I may have
to give a ball to one of the ushers," said Coach
Shinn.

"That's what I thought." Barrel hesitated. With the count two-and-nothing, the batter waited calmly. Dudas put the ball right over the center of the plate for a strike. Barrel was thinking that if the batter hadn't been taking, he would have knocked it out of the park. "What about Goodpasture?"

"Goodpasture's a southpaw."

"Don't give me that!" Barrel roared at the phone. "I saw him pitch batting practice Monday and he was throwing right."

"I tell you he throws left. I've been watching him out here all game long." Shinn turned to Harrison Goodpasture, who was sitting down. "Hey, Goodpasture, do you throw right-handed?"

Harrison smiled. "Whatever you say, Coach."

Sitting next to him, Danny mumbled, "Wait a minute—"

Coach Shinn looked puzzled, but turned back to the phone. "'You're right. I mean, he's right." On the mound, Dudas had thrown wide again. Shinn motioned for Goodpasture to start warming up again. He stood watching him to make sure he threw with his right. "I swear—"

The batter walked and Barrel popped out of the dugout like bread from a toaster. He signaled for his fifth pitcher. Goodpasture started toward the mound, but had to pass Danny. "Hey, wait a minute," his teammate stopped him. "Coach is right. You were throwing left-handed earlier."

Harrison grinned. "Remember what I told you about my switch pitch?"

"Are you trying to tell me—"

Harrison grasped his friend's hand. "Be cool, brother. Sit down and watch me humble this man who seeks to destroy us."

The next batter, Gonzales, stood in the batting circle as Harrison Goodpasture finished his warm-up throws. But at the last moment the other manager nodded for someone on the bench. One of the Cardinal reserves, Mark Lisak, rose and selected a bat from the rack. Gonzales returned to the dugout. The new batter moved to the batting circle and took several practice swings. Lisak was a left hander.

Kearney, the Cardinal manager, was playing percentages. A left-handed batter has an easier time hitting against a right-handed pitcher. He has more time to adjust to the flight of a ball curving toward him. The same with a right-handed batter against a left-handed pitcher.

But before the new batter stepped to the plate, Harrison gestured for time and walked toward the Cobra dugout. "Give me my other mitt," he asked.

Barrel Barnes looked down to where Harrison had dropped his jacket and spare mitt when he came in from the bullpen. He reached for the mitt, and paused. It was a mitt for a right hand, the kind used by a left-handed pitcher.

"That's the one," said Harrison.

Barrel handed him the mitt and took the one Harrison had brought to the mound. He gaped at it, because it was a mitt for a left hand, the kind used by a right-handed pitcher.

Catcher Ralph Pidcock walked to the mound to talk to Harrison. "One finger for a curve. Two fingers for a fastball," he said.

"We don't need any signals, man. I am going to throw the batter my eight-ball and he is going to break his back missing it."

"Yeah, well, one finger for a curve. Two fingers for a fastball. If I want an eight-ball I'll show you a fist." Pidcock returned to the plate, pulled his mask down over his face, and squatted.

Harrison looked over his shoulder at the runner on second, rocked, and followed through with a sweeping motion. The ball rolled lazily off the fingertips of his left hand and floated in an easy arc toward the plate where the batter coiled, ready to smash the pitch back at the pitcher. The batter rotated his shoulders, snapped his wrists, and brought his bat around with a mighty swing.

Wooosh, he missed. At the last moment the ball dipped as though it had fallen off a table. "*Stee-rahhh-kkk!*" said the umpire. But the catcher had missed the ball too. It went skittering between Pidcock's legs to roll back to the screen. Pidcock flipped off his mask and cap and ran to retrieve the ball, but by the time he got it the runners had advanced to second and third, putting the winning run in scoring position.

Standing at the edge of the dugout, Kearney, the Cardinal manager, scratched his head. I must be getting old, he thought. I send a left-handed hitter up to bat against a right-handed pitcher and it turns out the pitcher throws with his left.

In the Cobra dugout, Barrel Barnes stood motionless with his mouth hanging open. In the bullpen, Coach Shinn turned to Danny Wasocka. "Am I seeing right?"

"No, I think you're seeing left."

After Pidcock had retrieved the baseball, he snapped it peevishly back at his pitcher. He squatted and held one finger down below his mitt. Harrison shook his head. The catcher showed two fingers. Harrison again refused the sign. The catcher paused as though unwilling to go further. Harrison raised his left arm and made a fist.

Up in the press box, Blades of the *Tribune* turned to Holzman of the *Times*. "That rookie is pretty cocky for his first time on the mound."

With base runners on second and third, Harrison Goodpasture took a full windup, kicking his leg high overhead, his knuckles almost scraping the dirt of the mound, and then fired. Again the pitch soared over the plate—and darted upward. The batter wound himself into a circle trying to hit it. "*Stttt-ahhhh-reeee-akkkk!*" said the umpire, but this time the ball bounced off Pidcock's chest protector to roll down the first-base line.

Without hesitation the runner on third, who had come part way down the line with Harrison's windup, broke for the plate. Pidcock scrambled for the still spinning ball. Harrison came off the mound quick as lightning and sprinted to cover home plate. Pidcock reached the ball, grabbed it, and threw to Harrison just as the base runner came crashing home in a cloud of dust. Harrison snatched the ball from the air and put it on the runner. The umpire's thumb came up, the game was over, and the Cobras had won 4 to 3.

In the Cardinal dugout, Manager Kearney was burning. "I sure outguessed myself on that one," he mumbled. Up in the press box Blades turned to Holzman. "How do you spell that new pitcher's name?" In front of the Cobra dugout, Barrel Barnes had not moved and was still trying to figure it out. Danny ran in from the bullpen to congratulate his friend.

"I'd like to get this straight," Danny asked. "Are you left-handed or right-handed?"

"What you are looking at, my man," Harrison Goodpasture informed him, "is the only switch pitcher in baseball."

Here Comes the Judge

"The shame! Oh, the shame!" wailed Mama O'Leary. She clung to the bars of her cell at the city jail. "To think that I have sunk this low."

Sitting on a bench in the same cell was Laura Addison. "Relax, Mama," she advised. "We didn't do anything that wrong."

Mama wrung her hands and paced back and forth. "What would my late husband say if he could see me now—in jail like a common thief?"

"Mama, there was nothing common about what we did."

A matron arrived at the cell door and opened it. "The judge will see you now," she announced.

They followed the matron through a mass of corridors that led to a courtroom. Waiting were the other members of the Vipers who had been arrested. Also in the courtroom were Danny Wasocka, Harrison Goodpasture, and the Mayor's assistant, Napoleon Birdsong.

Danny edged over toward Laura. "There's good news and bad news," he said.

"Give me the good news first," said Laura.

"We won the game. The Cobras beat the Cardinals 4 to 3 and Harrison got the win."

"What's the bad news?"

Danny pointed toward the other side of the room where the Mayor's assistant stood. "Birdsong is here, and he wants the judge to throw the book at you."

"Does the judge have a good breaking pitch?"

"Listen, you won't think it so funny when you get sent away to prison for thirty years' hard labor."

"Will you come visit me?"

"Not on days when we're playing doubleheaders."

The bailiff rapped for attention and everybody stood. Judge Jason T. Ford strode into the courtroom, his long black robes flowing behind him. "Here comes the judge," whispered Harrison. Judge Ford glared out at his audience, then sat at the wide desk at the front of the courtroom. He nodded for everybody to be seated, and when they had done so, looked down at the pile of papers before him. He frowned.

"This is disgraceful," began the judge. "Disturbing the peace at City Hall. Loitering in the subway. Speeding on the expressway. And what's this that happened at the garbage dump?"

The Mayor's assistant smiled at the judge. "We'd rather you not refer to it as the garbage dump," said Birdsong. "That's Parkway Gardens."

"Well, whatever it is, it smells just as much," snorted Tongue.

"Silence!" The judge banged down his gavel. "We'll have order in the courtroom." He glared at Tongue. "Now what's this about the garbage— errr, Parkway Gardens?"

"The Mayor had gone there for a groundbreaking ceremony," explained Birdsong. "The minute His Honor stuck his shovel into the ground, he scraped it on a tin can."

"What do you expect to find in a garbage dump?" mumbled Tongue. "Buried treasure?"

The judge rapped his gavel again.

Birdsong continued, "The tin can had a message inside it saying s.o.s."

"That's the international code for help," commented the judge.

"It's also the slogan of this infernal group," snapped Birdsong, wagging his finger in the direction of the Vipers.

"Hmmm," said the judge, glancing again at the papers before him. "Continue with the charges. What's this next item about defiling the fire commissioner's birthday cake?"

"That was the Mayor's next stop. His Honor had gone to the Fire Academy to wish the commissioner a happy birthday. When they brought out the birthday cake, they discovered that somebody had written S.O.S. in strawberry-flavored letters on it."

"Strawberry-flavored letters," said the judge. "That's a serious offense."

"Wherever the Mayor goes," Birdsong complained, "these maniacs find some way to bother him."

"We don't want to bother the Mayor," Laura pleaded. "We just want to *talk* to him. We've been trying to get an appointment to see the Mayor for six months, but he's always too busy. Today was supposed to be See-the-People Day, but the only people the Mayor sees are those that Mr. Birdsong wants him to see. If we ever had a chance to talk to Mayor Wells for five minutes, maybe we at least could present our case. Even if he then said no, we could feel we had tried everything."

"And this S.O.S. slogan," asked the judge. "What does that mean?"

"It means Save Our Stadium. Stratton Field. We want to keep it. We don't want it destroyed just so the city can spend $50 million for some new plastic throw-away stadium that nobody wants."

"Won't the baseball fans of this city be mad if they don't get their new stadium?"

"*We* are the baseball fans of this city. We're

the ones who, win or lose, watch our team play every day. Not someone like Birdsong here, who never attends a game."

"That's not true," Napoleon Birdsong objected. "I go to the baseball game at least once a year—"

"To see the Mayor throw out the first ball on opening day," roared Tongue. "And then you go home. I'll bet you haven't sat past the third inning at one game in the last ten years!"

The Mayor's assistant turned red.

Laura turned back to the judge. "We don't want the new stadium built. It's cold and unfriendly. The hot dogs won't taste the same there. But more than that, we think it's totally unnecessary."

"Unnecessary?"

"Unnecessary!" Tongue repeated. "The city plans to spend $50 million to replace a baseball park that is perfectly adequate. Sure, Stratton Field is sixty years old, but that doesn't mean it has to be torn down."

"Besides," added Charmer, "old customs should be preserved. There should be at least one baseball park in the country where they still play the game on real grass. Where the scoreboard doesn't shoot off fireworks. Where you can still get in for a dollar. Where popcorn costs a dime. Where you can sit in the sun and watch a baseball game—*in the daylight.*"

"That's right," added Mama. "They want to put up light towers so they can play baseball games during the night. It'll attract mosquitoes."

"I never thought of that," said the judge.

Laura added, "We just think there are more important things that this city could spend its $50 million on than erecting a new baseball stadium just for a few rich box-seat holders."

Judge Ford leaned back in his seat and a dreamy look crossed his face. "When I was a boy my dad used to take me to Stratton Field during the summer to cheer for the Cobras. My dad's not with me now, and it's been a long, long time since I've visited the old place."

"Well, you better hurry," advised Tongue. "Only one more game is going to be played there."

"One more game," mused the judge.

"Then in come the bulldozers," sighed Charmer, "tearing, ripping, gauging, shoving, destroying, demolishing everything that once was so precious about our American heritage."

Napoleon Birdsong was becoming more and more angry. "Your Honor, these people have been charged with some serious offenses."

"Yes," said the judge, returning to reality. He directed himself to the Vipers. "Since this is the first offense for most of you, and I believe you have learned your lesson, I am placing you on probation. No more disruptions. No more dis-

figured birthday cakes. The minute I hear of
more trouble, you all go to jail. Case dismissed."
Judge Ford banged his gavel down on the desk
and, with a sweep of his black robes, rushed off
the stand, pausing at the door to his chambers.
"They're tearing down the old place. Hmmmm.
Too bad." Then he was gone.

Napoleon Birdsong gritted his teeth and
headed for the exit. Laura started after him. "Mr.
Birdsong. All summer long you have been prom-
ising us an appointment with the Mayor. Why
won't you let us talk to him?"

Birdsong turned, glared at her, then rushed
from the room.

Scorecard Sam moved to Laura's side:
"There's something fishy about that guy. There's
got to be another reason, besides pure stubborn-
ness, why he won't let us see the Mayor."

"He's just a prune," said Tongue.

"No, it's more than that," said Sam. "But I've
been through half the records in City Hall and
haven't found anything yet."

"Baseball records? In City Hall?"

"No, business records." Scorecard Sam started
to go.

Mama O'Leary laid a hand on Laura's shoulder. "We tried," said Mama, forcing a smile. "If
the Mayor had wanted to see us, he probably
would have done so. Besides, we can move the
pizzeria to some other location."

"But, Mama, it won't be the same."

"Nothing is ever the same. That's the nice thing about life. It's always changing. So we must change with it. Tomorrow is the last game of the season. I will go to the park and cheer for the Cobras."

"Mama," said Laura, delighted. "You've never attended a game before."

"Tomorrow will be the first time, and—" she said with a sigh, "—the last time."

But on Thursday there was no game. It rained. The Cardinals and Cobras were forced to postpone their showdown until Friday. But it did not rain in New York, and in that city later that evening, the Pirates lost. This gave the Cardinals the pennant. And it meant that the final game of the season, between the Cobras and the Cardinals, would have no effect on the standings.

Rest in Peace

"We have no excuse now not to start our rookies," insisted Coach Al Shinn the morning of the final game of the year.

"I think you're finally right," conceded Barrel Barnes. "You'll notice I said *finally*. The Pirates settled the issue by losing last night."

"I've just come from the visitors' dressing room," Shinn went on. "The Cardinal manager says he's pulling every one of his regulars to rest them for the divisional playoffs. His starting pitcher today was playing double-A ball two weeks ago."

"Can't blame him," said Barrel. "Still—"

"Still what? If they lose to us, it doesn't mean beans."

"There's such a thing as momentum. If you get used to losing, you continue to lose. We've won two games from the Cardinals. If I were managing that team I wouldn't want to ride into the playoff on a three-game losing streak." Barrel paused to think. "For the same reason, I'd like to end our season winning. It might become a habit."

"You're not thinking about playing *your* regulars?"

"Thinking about something and doing it are two different things," answered Barrel. "Arndt of the Expos went four-for-four last night. He's now only a half percentage point behind Pete Powers in the batting race. But the Expos are done for the year. All Pete has to do to win the title is not play today. All right—so I'll give Pete the day off and look at Martinez in right field." Barrel began making notes on his score sheet. "I'll play Dandridge at first, Elliot at shortstop, and Wasocka behind the plate. And I want to see if Goodpasture is for real. He only threw two pitches on Wednesday."

"I'll tell him to be ready." Coach Shinn started toward the locker room.

"Still—" added Barrel Barnes, "—the fans pay major league prices. They want the best you've got. I hate to have them cheated by watching what amounts to two minor league teams going through the motions."

"Don't be silly," laughed Shinn. "It's the last game of the season. It's the end of September. We're in last place and the race is all over. I'll pay you a dollar a head if more than five hundred fans come through the turnstiles today."

"No bet," said Barrel, and continued to pencil the names of the starters onto his score sheet.

But if Barrel had accepted the bet, he would have been at least forty thousand dollars richer that night. Even before Stratton Field's gates opened at 10:00 A.M., the fans began arriving to stand in line before the ticket windows. They carried Cobra pennants or purchased them at the gate. They brought home-made banners with messages like GO COBRAS GO! They wore Cobra caps, plastic and cloth, which in many cases had been dug from hiding places in attics and basements.

By 11:00 the lines in front of the ticket windows stretched clear to the streets. Traffic in those streets barely moved. By 12:30, an hour before game time, the ticket windows closed because no more seats remained to be sold. Those who arrived late had to visit nearby bars to watch the game on T.V., or turn around and go home. But many, even though they could not get in, still hung around to absorb the excitement.

Everybody had come to pay their last respects to Stratton Field, to see the ball park for one last time, to bid farewell to an old friend. Across the street, at the far end of the parking lot, more than a dozen cranes and bulldozers waited menacingly. Had not rain forced the one-day delay, they already would have been assaulting the baseball park.

In the club house Harrison Goodpasture was

sitting in front of his locker. Coach Shinn passed. "How's the arm today, Goodpasture?"

Harrison looked up at the coach, a twinkle in his eyes. "Which one, Coach?"

"You're probably the only pitcher in the world who would ask that question. Let's start with the left."

"Left arm feels all right."

"And the other arm?"

"The right arm feels all left."

"Well, they both better be ready, because Barrel says you're the starting pitcher in today's game."

"Yeah," said Harrison as Coach Shinn headed out of the field. *"Yeah!"* he shouted, and picked up his mitts to follow.

A few minutes later Barrel Barnes walked into the locker room to post the starting lineup on the bulletin board. Catcher Ralph Pidcock approached him. "I understand you're thinking about pitching Goodpasture."

"Not thinking about it, Ralph, doing it."

"The kid's tough," said Pidcock, "but he makes me look bad with those junk pitches he throws. The batters can't tell which way that ball is going to jump, but neither can I. And he throws so slow, the other team will steal him blind."

"Don't worry, Ralph," Barrel smiled wryly. "I'm using Wasocka behind the plate today. If there are any passed balls or stolen bases, they'll go against his record."

Pidcock hesitated. "I don't mind catching the rookie. It's just that I wanted you to know the problems."

"I know the problems, Ralph," said Barrel. He turned to Pete Powers, who was sitting in front of his locker with a worried look on his face. "Pete, I'm handing you the batting title. Take the day off."

Pete looked relieved. "I appreciate that, Skip. I really do."

Danny Wasocka grabbed his catching gear and started for the door. When he stepped from the club house to the outfield, he suddenly felt weak. He realized he was surrounded by forty thousand fans. He was about to start his first major league game before what probably was the biggest crowd of the year at Stratton Field.

Danny glanced into the bleachers and, despite the crowd, immediately located Laura Addison sitting in the front row. He was surprised to see her wearing a black armband as though there had been a death in the family. She waved. Danny waved back and was about to shout and ask her about the armband when he realized everyone else in the bleachers wore similar black armbands. Then he saw the banner tied to the fence behind the catwalk and understood why. The banner said:

REST IN PEACE
STRATTON FIELD

It was the last game that ever would be played in Stratton Field and the Vipers were in mourning.

Danny walked toward the bullpen where Collins, the other catcher, was receiving Harrison Goodpasture's warm-up pitches. Danny was aware of a constant low rumble caused by the presence of so many people in one place. The rumble was like the sound of the ocean, out of which you occasionally would hear a spoken voice, a shouted name, a vendor selling popcorn.

Several fans leaned over the wall and thrust programs at Danny. He signed several, then realized he had better move on. Usually Barrel would station one or two reserves next to the bullpen wall to sign autographs. That kept the fans happy so they wouldn't bother the starting pitcher trying to warm up. But today many of the reserves were starting.

He tapped Collins on the shoulder and the other catcher rose to let Danny take his place. Harrison had been throwing easily. He now held the baseball over his head and waved it as though trying to shake something from its surface. "This is my hunker ball," he announced. He threw a lob that followed an arc which at its high point rose to nearly fifteen feet off the ground. Then it dropped nearly straight down into Danny's mitt.

"Why do you call that your hunker ball?" asked Danny as he returned the ball.

"Because it just *hunkers* over the plate and dares the batter to hit it." Harrison next threw sidearm and the ball seemed to flutter twice before settling into Danny's mitt. "That's my butter ball. I only throw it at overweight batters."

Coach Shinn stood by Harrison's side observing his delivery with wonder. "Almost game time, Goodpasture," said Shinn. "Better start throwing hard."

"Hard? I am throwing hard, Coach. What you see is what you got. People have been known to pass my fastball walking. I'm the only man alive who can kill a fly on a windowpane with a thrown pitch and not break that window."

At that moment Danny became aware that the constant rumble of noise had changed in tone. Some of the crowd seemed angry. They began to boo. Then the boos increased in volume. People began to stand to see the reason for the booing.

Walking down the aisle toward a front-row box seat was Mayor E. Forrest Wells III. Along with him came football coach Stanley Stark and several other people who looked important, although Danny didn't know their names. At the end of the line came the Mayor's assistant, Napoleon Birdsong.

The Mayor reached his seat and waited for his assistant. "Why all the booing?" asked His Honor.

Birdsong knew the reason for the booing. He could see that many of those standing and booing also wore S.O.S. buttons, but he didn't want to call the Mayor's attention to that. "They're booing the umpires," suggested Birdsong, even though the umpires had not yet taken the field.

"Oh, of course," said the Mayor. He settled into his seat and the booing decreased. "I don't see any umpires."

"Baseball fans just like to boo," grumbled Stark. "At a baseball game, what else do they have to do?"

The Mayor turned to Birdsong. "Now let's see, we're supposed to throw out the first ball."

"No, that was taken care of last spring." Birdsong consulted a notebook. "After the game we'll have a short ceremony with a shovel."

"A shovel?"

"You're to dig up home plate so that it can be replanted in the new stadium next year."

"Good," said Mayor Wells. "We should have respect for the old traditions." He looked around at the others with him in the box seat and everybody nodded in agreement except Stanley Stark.

At that moment a roar erupted from the crowd. The Cobras ran from the dugout to take their positions on the field.

Gryzbacz at the Bat

Harrison Goodpasture moved onto the mound carrying two mitts: one for his right hand, the other for his left. He scraped the dirt in front of the pitching rubber with his spikes until he was satisfied with the footing. He walked to the rear of the mound and dropped the mitt for the left hand onto the edge of the grass. Since the Cardinal lead-off man batted right-handed, Harrison planned to pitch right-handed against him. He took two more warm-up throws, then nodded to the umpire that he was ready to begin.

"Play ball!" shouted the umpire, and the cry echoed through the hushed stadium.

The batter moved forward, anchored his feet in the batter's box, and waved his bat across the plate. Danny Wasocka squatted and held two fingers below his mitt, the signal for a curve. Harrison nodded, wound up, and threw.

Thunnnk! The ball curved into Danny's mitt

as the batter watched it go past for a called strike.

Kearney, the Cardinal manager, stood on the edge of the dugout rubbing the back of his neck. "Now wait a minute," he said to one of his players. "Isn't that the same rookie pitcher who finished the game against us two days ago?"

The player glanced at the lineup taped to the wall of the dugout. "That's the man." Harrison's second pitch was wide outside for a ball.

"Either I'm losing my mind, or that rook has a twin brother who looks exactly like him. Because the pitcher on Wednesday threw left-handed." The batter swung at the next pitch and sent an easy grounder to Elliot at shortstop for the first out.

The second batter also batted right-handed. He missed the first pitch, fouled off another, then flied out to center. But the third batter, Welch, a reserve outfielder, swung from the other side of the plate.

Welch watched the second out while standing in the batting circle, then rapped the handle of his bat on the ground to knock loose the weight he had been using with his practice swings. He moved forward, swinging his bat left-handed. Goodpasture looked at him briefly, then turned to the back of the mound where he had dropped his other glove. He picked it up and put it on his right hand, leaving the other mitt in its place.

Harrison nodded at the sign from Danny, three fingers for a flutterball. He rocked and threw—with his left hand.

Welch stared at the pitch as it fluttered across the plate for a called strike, then shook his head as though he had been stung on the back of the neck by a bee. "Huh?" he said. Danny snapped the ball quickly back to Harrison.

Harrison threw again and once more the Cardinal batter watched the pitch float over the center of the plate. "Strike two!"

Welch looked blankly at the umpire. "Something's wrong," he said.

"It was a perfect strike," the umpire replied.

In the Cardinal dugout, Manager Kearney had taken two steps up the stairs of his dugout, then halted as though uncertain what to do.

Harrison pitched once more. *"Hee-rawwwk-hreee!"* cried the umpire, jerking his thumb high to indicate the batter had struck out. Welch, who still had not moved the bat from his shoulder, now took two steps backward and let it slip from his hands. "Wait a minute," he said again, still uncertain what bothered him.

But the Cardinal manager knew, and this time came charging out of the dugout toward home plate, shouting and gesturing angrily in the direction of Harrison Goodpasture. "He's pitching wrong!" roared Manager Kearney.

The umpire stared straight-faced back at the

manager. "Looks more like your man is batting wrong."

"No, he pitched left-handed. Against the first two batters, he pitched right-handed."

The umpire glared at him. "Are you trying to tell me that there are two pitchers out there on the mound? I only saw one."

Barrel Barnes approached to see what the argument was about. The Cardinal manager turned on him. "Barrel, first your pitcher's throwing right, then he's throwing left. What is he?"

"He's a switch pitcher. I haven't figured it out entirely myself. All I know is, so far, he gets people out."

Manager Kearney stood stunned, as though the entire idea was foreign to his idea of how the game should be played.

"Gentlemen," said the umpire. "I don't know whether that pitcher is human or not, but I do know this is the 164th game of the year. Let's get it over with. Play ball."

The Cardinal manager returned to his dugout, sadly shaking his head in wonderment, and waved his team out into the field. "Switch pitcher," he mumbled. "Switch batters I can understand, but a switch pitcher?" Manager Kearney suddenly stopped and snapped his fingers. "Wait a minute—when does Gryzbacz come to bat?"

One of his players glanced at the lineup on the wall. "He's batting eighth."

Manager Kearney cackled. "We'll see what that switch pitcher does with him."

Up in the box seats, Mayor Wells turned to Stanley Stark. "Goodness, what was that all about?"

"Baseball people are always arguing," grumbled Stark. "They ought to at least keep the clock running so we can get home sooner."

And in the bleachers, Laura Addison turned to Mama O'Leary, who was attending her first baseball game. "Did you see that, Mama? Harrison Goodpasture is a switch pitcher."

Mama clucked her tongue. "And he seemed like such a nice boy."

The Cobra hitters went down in order during their half of the first. Goodpasture walked one batter in the second, but he didn't advance. The Cobras again failed to hit. The Cardinals came to bat again in the third. "Gryzbacz, you know what to do!" Manager Kearney instructed his first batter, a utility infielder who was playing shortstop that day.

"Right, Skip."

"Right *and* left, Gryzbacz," said the manager.

Gryzbacz moved toward the plate swinging his bat in slow circles over his head. Barrel noticed the batter approaching and suddenly smiled. "Oh, oh. We're in for some fun."

"What's up?" asked Coach Shinn.

"Tell me, what side of the plate does Gryzbacz bat from?"

Shinn saw the point and grinned. Up in the bleachers, Tongue also understood what was about to happen. "Hey, Gryzbacz is a switch batter."

"And Goodpasture is a switch pitcher," said Charmer.

Tongue chortled with delight. "Switch batter meets switch pitcher. This should be the biggest showdown since Frankenstein battled the Wolf Man."

"Be respectful," said Scorecard Sam. "Baseball history is about to be made."

Harrison Goodpasture looked toward Gryzbacz, who had taken his place on the side nearest Danny Wasocka's right arm. Harrison bent to pick up his right mitt so he could pitch left-handed. When he looked back at the plate, Gryzbacz had moved to the left side.

Harrison retrieved his first mitt, but then Gryzbacz returned to the right side of the plate.

"Play ball! Play ball!" said the umpire with irritation. In the stands, laughter began to fill the air.

"Tell the batter to stop moving!" snapped Harrison.

"Tell the pitcher to quit playing with his mitts!" countered Gryzbacz.

"Fellows. Fellows," said the umpire. "This is the 164th game of the year. Let's get it over with."

Harrison again reached for his right mitt and Gryzbacz once more shifted to the left side of the plate. Some of the laughter in the stands began to turn to boos. Harrison threw down the right mitt and picked up the left one, but before Gryzbacz could switch, the Cardinal manager popped out of the dugout and charged the umpire. "He's in violation of the rules," said Manager Kearney. "Too much baggage on the field."

The umpire agreed. "Goodpasture, you'll have to get rid of one of those mitts."

Harrison frowned, but flung his right mitt toward the dugout. Barrel fielded it and made a move onto the field to protest the decision, but decided against it.

The umpire pointed sternly at the batter. "Pick one side of the plate and stay on it until the pitcher releases the pitch."

Manager Kearney charged the umpire. "I'm playing this game under protest."

"Protest?" snarled the umpire. "This is the 164th game of the season. When do you plan to replay it—during the Christmas holidays?"

The Cardinal manager scowled, but returned to his dugout.

The pitcher and batter again faced each other. Harrison, mitt on his left hand, stood ready to throw. Gryzbacz moved to the right side of the plate.

Harrison took the mitt off his left hand and put it on his right, his thumb stuffed into the place normally reserved for his little finger. Gryzbacz moved to the left.

Harrison moved his mitt to his left hand. Gryzbacz moved to the right.

"Fellows, this is the 164th game of the season."

Harrison moved his mitt to his right hand. Gryzbacz moved to the left.

"That batter is delaying the game!" shouted Barrel from his dugout.

Harrison moved his mitt to his left hand. Gryzbacz moved to the right.

"That pitcher is delaying the game!" shouted Manager Kearney.

Up in the box seats, Stanley Stark rumbled impatiently, "The referee ought to penalize them both fifteen yards."

Gryzbacz returned to the right side of the plate. Danny signaled Harrison with three fingers. The pitcher shook his head. Danny showed two fingers. Harrison shook off the sign again. Danny put four fingers under his mitt, the sign for the hunker ball. Harrison nodded. He kicked his left leg high and reached back with his arm, almost dragging his knuckles on the ground, then threw with a long, lazy, overhead motion that catapulted the baseball high over the batter's head.

The crowd gasped. The pitch went up twenty feet, thirty feet, forty feet, hung suspended as though filled with helium, then dropped like a rock, picking up speed as it went.

Clunk! It landed on the plate. The umpire stared at the baseball as though uncertain what to do. Then he lifted his right arm. *"Steeee-rawwww!"*

Gryzbacz backed out of the batter's box. "What do you mean strike? It landed on the plate!"

"It passed through the strike zone to get there," growled the umpire. "Strike one. Play ball."

Gryzbacz grumbled, but moved to the left side of the plate. Harrison shifted his mitt to the other hand. This time he shook off three signs until Danny again put four fingers down for the hunker ball. Once more it took off like a Saturn rocket, floated, and came plummeting down onto the plate. *Clunk!* For a moment Gryzbacz looked as though he was ready to smash the baseball as it lay there, but he did not. *"Heeee-ryyyy!"* roared the umpire. The fans cheered.

"If this were the Astrodome, he couldn't throw that pitch," Gryzbacz complained. "It would hit the roof."

"This isn't the Astrodome," said the umpire. "Strike two."

Gryzbacz paused as though in deep thought. "What did you tell me—to stay on one side until the pitcher releases the pitch?"

"You know the rules."

"But we seem to be breaking new ground today."

"Play ball!"

This time Gryzbacz remained on the left side of the plate. Harrison shook off nearly a half-dozen signs before finally agreeing to one. Out in the bleachers, Tongue screamed in a voice that could be heard all the way to the press box, "Feed him the big high one!"

Harrison wound up as he had before, but just as he released the pitch, Gryzbacz suddenly started to leap from the left to the right side of the plate. But Harrison hadn't thrown his hunker ball. He had thrown his fastball. Just as Gryzbacz crossed the plate going west to east, the pitch came whistling across going north to south.

Tee-wakkkkk! It struck him on the batting helmet. Gryzbacz crumpled in a heap.

The umpire stared down at the batter as he lay on the ground, shocked, speechless, as though the day's events had been too much for him and he didn't know what to do next.

Barrel Barnes ran from his dugout toward the plate. "The batter jumped in front of the pitch. He's out."

The umpire continued to stare at the fallen batsman.

The Cardinal manager also ran to the plate. "What do you mean he's out?"

"He left the batter's box!" shouted Barrel.

"The umpire told him to stay put until the pitcher released the ball. He didn't say anything about afterward."

Up in the box seats, Mayor Wells turned to Coach Stark. "What's happening now?"

"I think they call that intentional grounding," said Stark.

"Safe!" shouted Kearney.

"Out!" shrieked Barrel.

Finally the umpire spoke. "I've made my decision. The batter is awarded first base, but he's out."

"That's impossible!" shouted the two managers at once.

The umpire pointed at Gryzbacz, still lying bleary-eyed on the ground. "He's out. He's unconscious. I'm awarding him first base for being hit with a pitched ball, but you better get a stretcher, and please, gentlemen, remember that this is the 164th game of the year."

Pop-up

After they helped Gryzbacz, dazed but otherwise unhurt, back to the dugout, the Cardinal manager sent in Dave Ayars, another reserve, as a pinch runner.

Harrison Goodpasture stood staring at the base runner for a moment, then returned his attention to the plate. The next batter was Mike Hack, the Cardinal pitcher and a weak hitter.

Danny walked to the mound to talk to Harrison. "He's going to be bunting, so pitch him high and inside." Harrison nodded as though he already knew what to do, and Danny trotted back to the plate.

Harrison nodded at Danny's sign, glanced at the runner on first, and threw without a windup. Wynder, the third baseman, expecting a sacrifice, had set himself far in front of his normal position. Dandridge, the first baseman, charged toward the plate with the pitch. Second baseman

Murray moved over to cover first while Elliot, the shortstop, headed for second in case of a play at that base. Ayars the Cardinal base runner, also began his sprint for second.

But the pitch was too high and the umpire called, *"Ball one."*

Again the ballplayers resumed their roles like actors in some play: the sign from the catcher, the glance by the pitcher, the base runner moving, the infielders charging, the pitch.

Hack squared to bunt. *Tik!* The pitch struck his bat and dribbled down the third-base line. Reacting instantly, Danny flipped off his mask and sprang after the ball, which was rolling parallel with the white chalk mark. Wynder, the third baseman, also was moving full speed toward the rolling baseball while the runner Ayars sprinted for second. The ball began to roll across the white line.

Danny reached the ball, grabbed it, and saw out of the corner of his eye that he had time to catch the runner at second. He spun and threw, a rifle shot direct into Elliot's mitt, a foot off the ground and a foot to the first-base side of second. Elliot merely had to hold his mitt in that position and the runner slid right into it. Danny grinned as he saw the second-base umpire jerk his thumb in the air, indicating the runner was out.

Then Danny heard the home-plate umpire behind him announce, *"Foul ball."* The ball had

rolled from fair into foul territory just as Danny
had picked it up, so the runner was not out. He
would go back to first and they would begin over
again.

Danny retrieved his mitt from the dust and
settled behind the plate. Harrison threw and the
batter squared to bunt again, but the pitch broke
upward and Hack fouled the ball into the seats.

"Strike two," said the umpire.

With a two-strike count the batter would be
out if he bunted foul again, so the infielders
moved back almost to their normal positions.
Danny knew that most pitchers were poor hitters
and thus more likely to take a chance on a third-
strike sacrifice, so he still remained alert. But on
the next pitch Hack was swinging as though he
wanted to hit the baseball out of the park. He
fouled the pitch deep into the left-field grandstand.

Again the drama began. Harrison glanced toward first, began to throw, and at that instant the
runner broke for second. He's stealing, thought
Danny, and as the pitch from Harrison came
floating toward the plate Danny readied himself
to grab the ball, stride, and throw out the runner.
But in the last instant Hack raised his bat in the
pitch's path, dumping a bunt that fell between
home plate and the pitcher's mound.

Danny lunged forward at the same time Harrison charged off the mound. Again Danny

reached the ball first as it lay dead in the grass, and cocked his arm to throw to second. But Ayars, who had gotten a good jump on the pitch, already was beginning his slide, and Danny knew it was too late to get him. Instead, he relaxed and threw easily to Dandridge at first, accepting the sacrifice. The Cobras now had one out, but the Cardinals had a runner in scoring position on second with the top of their batting order up.

The next batter stepped up to the plate and on a two-and-one count, whacked the ball soundly, sending it high and deep to right field. The fans gasped as though fearful it might be a home run, but the baseball dropped short. Martinez caught it with his back almost to the wall. The fans let out a sigh. Ayars tagged at second and dashed toward third base. He went in standing as Martinez took no chances on a run-scoring error and threw to the mound.

A new batter stepped to the plate and Danny walked out to the mound to talk to his pitcher. "Listen, nothing fancy. No eight-ball pitches. If the ball gets away from me, Hotfoot over there will be sitting in the dugout before I retrieve it."

"How about a big, sloppy, right-handed curve?"

"Perfect. But remember to cover the plate."

Harrison threw the curve, but it was wide for a ball. Danny called for a slider, but it was low.

Ball two. Ayars made motions as though he might steal home, but Harrison watched him closely.

Again Danny wanted a curve, and this time it came rotating over the heart of the plate. The batter swung, but at the last instant the path of the baseball flattened. The batter tried to correct, but he had swung under the pitch.

Tunk! The struck ball caromed upward, a high pop-up. With one swipe of his hand, Danny sent his mask and cap bouncing backwards over his shoulder. He sprung to his feet and began to follow the path of the still rising ball with his eyes. The pop-up reached its high point, then began to drift downwards, pushed by a wind from the outfield. Danny sprinted under it to the edge of the box-seat wall. He placed his right hand on the wall and leaned out into the boxes, ready to stab for the ball with his mitt hand. Out of the corner of one eye Danny saw that one of the fans in that box had risen and was looking up, apparently ready to fight him for the ball.

The ball came down and Danny lunged at it, colliding with the fan as he did so. The baseball plopped into his mitt and stuck for the second out.

The fan fell backwards, tumbling over his chair and crashing to the ground. Danny suddenly realized it was Stanley Stark. "I thought I signaled for a fair catch," said Stark groggily.

"Sorry," Danny apologized, glancing back toward the diamond to check Ayars on third. He looked again in the box seats, embarrassed that he had knocked someone down even if it was Stanley Stark. Another person was standing over the downed football coach. He looked very familiar. "Holy cow, it's the Mayor," Danny gulped.

"It's a pleasure to meet you, young man," said E. Forrest Wells III, extending his hand as though to ask for Danny's vote. Danny looked at the Mayor's hand, then looked at the baseball in his own hand. "Would you like to keep this baseball?"

"Oh, thanks," said the Mayor, reaching for the ball. "I may need one to throw out the first game of the next season."

"*Danny!*"

Danny Wasocka quickly turned. Harrison Goodpasture was sprinting off the mound, shouting his name. "*Danny!*" Ayars had broken for the plate.

Danny pulled the baseball out of the Mayor's grasp and fired it to his friend. Harrison took the throw standing in the base path and turned to see Ayars bearing down on him like a tidal wave. The two collided and there was a cloud of dust. Harrison, the ball still in his hand, tumbled over the runner. Rolling and bouncing up, the ball was still in his hand. He looked hopefully at the umpire.

The umpire stood poised for a moment, bent

forward, staring into the dust as though trying to
replay the scene in his mind before announcing
his decision. Finally he jerked his thumb in the
air. *"Rr-rr-rr-rrr-owwww!"* The batter was out
and the side was retired without the run scoring.

Danny breathed a sigh of relief and turned
back to the Mayor. "One of my friends has been
trying to reach you all week."

"I'm always available," smiled Mayor Wells.
"Once a week I travel through the city and see
the people."

"Maybe so, but you're not seeing all of the
people. My friends, some real baseball fans,
tried to talk to you and got thrown in jail."

Napoleon Birdsong, who was sitting behind
the Mayor, leaned forward to whisper in his ear.
"He's talking about that group of maniacs that
caused you all the trouble yesterday.

"That's right," agreed Stanley Stark. "They're
those anti-stadium nuts."

"Those anti-stadium nuts will cost you the
baseball vote if you listen to them," warned
Birdsong.

"That's not true," said Danny. "The true baseball fans sit out in the bleachers. They want to
keep Stratton Field, not tear it down. I'll bet if
you started to ask all the other people who came
to the game today, you'd find that nobody else
wants a new stadium either. Why do you think
you got booed the minute you walked in?"

"I thought they were booing the umpires."

"The fans love the umpires. It's you they don't like. There are forty thousand people sitting here today who will vote against you in the next election because you wrecked their ball park."

Mayor Wells grimaced. "I never thought of it that way." He shifted his gaze toward his assistant. "Is this true, Birdsong?"

But at that moment the voice of Barrel Barnes sounded from the dugout. "Wasocka! Are you playing this game or are you collecting autographs?"

Danny realized he was batting next. He bagan to strip off his shin pads. He looked back at the Mayor, but saw he was talking to Napoleon Birdsong. Danny ran to the dugout to get his bat.

Field Goal

Danny Wasocka pulled his bat from the rack and strode to the mound. He reached down into the dirt to rub some on his hands. Then he stretched, stepped to the plate, patted his batting helmet down tight on his head, and swung his bat two or three times to loosen his muscles.

Then he struck out.

In the dugout, Barrel Barnes groaned. The rookie almost costs him a run in the top of the inning. Now he reaches like a sucker for an outside curve ball on the third strike. Barrel wondered if he made a mistake putting so many rookies in the lineup.

"Don't say it," said Coach Shinn. "I know what you're thinking."

In the meantime, Mayor Wells had left his box seat and was striding up the ramp over left field that led to the bleachers. "I don't know if you should go there," cautioned Birdsong, who was running to keep up with him. "Those people are dangerous."

"Nonsense," said the Mayor. "They're just good fans."

"But—"

"No buts, Birdsong. That catcher was right: I've allowed myself to become separated from the true citizens of this fair city."

"We have See-the-People Day every Wednesday," suggested Birdsong.

"Oh, I see people and they see me, but I don't meet them. There's never any real contact." Mayor Wells looked over his shoulder and glared at his assistant. "Sometimes I think that's the way you want it." Birdsong blanched.

A blue-uniformed usher was guarding the ramp leading from grandstand to bleachers. He recognized the Mayor and lifted a rope to let him pass. Before Birdsong could follow, however, the usher dropped the rope.

Mayor Wells strode up the ramp to the bleachers. He gazed over the crowd jammed shoulder to shoulder on the backless seats. They seemed almost to be sitting on each other's laps. The aisles were full. Some bleacher patrons had climbed the chain fence and hung from it like bats on a cave wall, staring out at the game. The crowd groaned as Dandridge, the rookie first baseman, struck out to end the inning. The Cardinals trotted in from the field for their turn at bat.

Mayor Wells spotted a familiar face among those standing behind the last row of seats. "Judge Ford, what are you doing here?"

The judge seemed as surprised to see the Mayor as the Mayor had been to see him. "I learned that this would be the last game ever played in Stratton Field," he explained. "I was reminded of all the fun I had here as a boy. My dad took me to Cobra baseball games when I was in grade school."

"My father did too," admitted the Mayor, who was twenty years younger than the judge.

"A lot of happy days," Judge Ford recalled. "A lot of great players played here. Ty Cobb. Rogers Hornsby. Grover Cleveland Alexander. Hack Wilson. Babe Ruth hit home runs here. He once signaled to the stands that he was going to knock one out of here, then did it. This park is like a historical monument."

"I suppose so," agreed the Mayor. "It does seem a shame to tear down Stratton Field. But we can't disappoint the fans."

"Disappoint the fans? The fans want to keep Stratton Field."

"I didn't know that."

"Nearly two dozen of them were brought into my court yesterday for disturbing the peace. They were protesting the plans to tear down Stratton Field."

"Is that what they were protesting against?"

asked the Mayor. "I didn't realize what they were saying. There are so many protest groups coming at you these days that sometimes you lose track of who is protesting what." The Mayor turned as though he wanted to tell his assistant something, but Napoleon Birdsong was no longer at his side.

The fans sprung suddenly to their feet as the Cardinal batter hit a sharp line drive straight to the outfield for what looked like an extra-base hit. Harmon, the center fielder, caught the ball on the run. The fans sighed and sat down.

Judge Ford beckoned for the Mayor to follow him. He led down the steps to the first row of the bleachers. "Mayor Wells, I'd like you to meet Mama O'Leary."

Mama O'Leary turned around in her seat and gasped, "Mama Mia. It's His Honor himself."

Down on the field, the Cobras came to bat in the bottom of the fourth. Martinez, who had replaced Pete Powers in right field, opened with a sharp single down the third-base line. Harmon hit a blooper that dropped in front of the left fielder. But with men on first and second, the next three batters failed to hit and the score remained 0 to 0.

The first Cardinal batter up in the fifth inning changed that. He connected with one of Harrison Goodpasture's pitches that dipsied when it should have doodled. The ball flew off the bat and forty thousand fans watched in complete silence as it sailed into the left-field bleachers where the Mayor now sat with Mama O'Leary and the Vipers. One of the bleacher fans picked up the baseball after it had bounced down off the wire fence and threw it back onto the playing field.

"Don't the fans usually keep baseballs hit into the stands for souvenirs?" asked the Mayor.

"No respectable Cobra fan wants anything to do with an enemy home run," explained Tongue.

"My goodness," said Mayor Wells. "That's what I call team loyalty."

"We're loyal to this stadium, too," prodded Laura. "That's why we don't want it torn down."

"Tell me more."

On the field, Barrel Barnes watched from the dugout as Harrison Goodpasture, after having given up the home run, walked the next batter on five pitches. Barrel motioned to the umpire for time-out and walked to the mound. Danny Wasocka joined them. "How are the pitches coming across the plate?" Barrel asked Danny.

"That guy who hit the homer simply made a good guess," Danny replied.

Barrel looked at Harrison. "Then worry about the next batter, not the last one."

Harrison nodded, got the batter to tap an easy roller to the mound. Hack, the pitcher, batted next and looked at a called third strike, retiring the side.

"Next year I'll have plenty of time to learn about baseball games," Mama was telling Mayor Wells. "They're going to tear down my pizzeria because of the new stadium."

"But aren't they building the new stadium on the site of the old one?" the Mayor asked.

"They're doing that," interrupted Laura, "but they're building a parking lot on the site of O'Leary's Pizzeria. That's why she's upset."

"And the reason we're upset," added Tongue, "is because we don't think the city needs to spend $50 million for a stadium the people don't need, don't want, but still have to pay for."

"There's an even better reason to be upset," said a voice from behind.

Everybody turned to see Scorecard Sam standing in the aisle with a sheet of paper in his hand. "I'm late for the game because I've spent the last two days digging in the records at City Hall. I think the Mayor should learn what I found."

Scorecard Sam waved the sheet of paper. "We should be upset because of who stands to profit from the new stadium. Only one company bid on the right to run the parking lots. The city council approved the bid without debate. I have the list of stockholders in that company."

"Let me see that list," said the Mayor.

"You'll notice a familiar name," said Scorecard Sam, handing the list to the Mayor.

"Napoleon Birdsong!" gasped Judge Ford, who was reading over the Mayor's shoulder.

"That stuffed prune!" Tongue made a fist. "No wonder he never would let us see the Mayor."

"I'm shocked," said Mayor Wells.

Scorecard Sam handed another piece of paper to the Mayor. "And here's the list of owners of the contracting company whose bulldozers are waiting outside to tear this place apart. You won't find Birdsong's name on the list—only that of his brother-in-law."

"This is an outrage!" said the Mayor. He turned to look for his assistant. "Birdsong! What's the meaning of this?" But Napoleon Birdsong was nowhere in sight.

Mayor E. Forrest Wells III rose from his seat. He looked at the rows of fans surrounding him. "I want to thank you for bringing this to my attention," he began. "I'm sorry it took you so long to reach me. I think all of us now know why. Judge—" the Mayor nodded at Judge Ford, "—I think you and I have some talking to do before this game is over."

Charmer lumbered to his feet and climbed onto the outfield wall. He threw back his head and blew a few notes on his flute.

"STRIKE!" roared the Vipers.

On the field, however, the Cobras seemed

to be having little luck. Danny grounded out to start the fifth inning. Elliot, the shortstop, walked, but Goodpasture struck out and Dandridge lined to the pitcher.

The Cobras went down in order in the sixth, left two men stranded in the seventh, and failed again in the eighth. Harrison matched the Cardinal pitcher's record, but the Cobras still trailed 1 to 0.

Then Murray led off in the bottom of the ninth with a single between second and third. While taking his practice swings, Danny watched the third-base coach. The coach rubbed his palm across the front of his uniform; the sign for a sacrifice.

The first pitch was outside for a ball. The next pitch came across the plate letter high and Danny squared to meet it with both hands on the bat. *Dunk!* He bunted the ball down the third-base line. The third baseman charged. The pitcher and catcher also rushed to field the ball. All three suddenly stopped.

Danny sprinted across first base, having drawn no throw. Murray slid safely into second. "Foul ball," announced the umpire. Danny's sacrifice bunt had rolled to a stop barely outside the foul line.

Danny returned to the plate and picked up his bat. The pitcher threw and Danny squared again. *Dunk!* His bunt rolled down the third-base line.

He again crossed first base not having drawn a throw. But the umpire at second was calling Murray out. The baseball had been struck too sharply, and the third baseman had fielded it in time to force the runner. One out.

Elliot, the rookie shortstop, had been standing in the batter's cage, but now Barrel Barnes called him back to the dugout. He didn't want to take a chance on another inexperienced young player. He selected Archer to hit in Elliot's place. Archer dumped a perfect bunt between the pitcher and the first baseman, and Danny slid safely into second base. Archer was thrown out at first for out number two. Danny rose and brushed the dust from his uniform, looking toward the dugout to see what Barrel's next move would be. Harrison Goodpasture would be next to bat, but Danny was certain there would be another batter.

Barrel already had decided to use a pinch hitter. One out separated them from ending the season in defeat. The only question was who? He finally pointed his finger at Ralph Pidcock.

"No way!" came a loud voice from the other end of the dugout.

Barrel was stunned that somebody would challenge him.

"*No way!*" said the voice, this time more loudly. Pete Powers had risen from his seat and was selecting a bat from the rack. "No way you are going to send Ralph Pidcock to bat in the last of the ninth when you have your best batter, me, sitting on the bench. No way." Pete Powers walked jauntily past Pidcock and gave him a large smile. "No offense, Ralph."

Barrel glared at Pete Powers. "That pitcher throws southpaw and I want a right-handed batter up against him."

Pete pushed his face within a few inches of that of his manager and flashed a big grin. "Skip, I don't care if that pitcher drop-kicks the ball across the plate, I'm still going to knock him out of that box."

"What about your batting title?" Barrel shouted after Pete Powers, who stepped out of the dugout swinging his bat over his head.

Pete Powers' reply could barely be heard beneath the roar from the fans. "I'll still win the title, because the next pitch is landing clear out of this park."

And it did. The home run that won the last game of the season for the Cobras cleared the screen in right field still going up. And if a football referee had been present in the new stadium next door, he would have raised two hands in the air, because the baseball finally came down through one of Stanley Stark's goalposts.

The Golden Shovel

Stanley Stark, who had fallen asleep somewhere in the middle of the fifth inning, was suddenly awakened by the roar that followed Pete Powers' game-winning home run. "Game over?" he mumbled. "Game over? Let's get that plate-digging ceremony done with." Ignoring the baseball players who had converged on Pete Powers as he crossed home plate, Stark pushed his way onto the field.

"Where's the Mayor?" grumbled Stark. "I've got some football films I want to view tonight."

Mayor Wells appeared in left field followed by Judge Ford. The crowd, so happy over the sudden victory, forgot to boo him as he walked across one of the few remaining fields in the major leagues that had to be trimmed with a lawnmower.

The Mayor moved to a microphone that had been placed near home plate. A groundskeeper appeared with a golden shovel. "Ladies and Gentlemen," Mayor Wells began. "You came to Stratton Field today thinking you would see the last game ever played here."

There was an undercurrent of grumbles. Mayor Wells continued, "I thought so too, and I'm about to be handed a golden shovel so that I can dig up home plate for replanting in the new $50-million stadium."

The grumbles grew louder, and this time there were boos.

The Mayor took the golden shovel from the groundskeeper, looked at it, and threw it down. "But I'm not going to use the shovel."

There was a sudden gasp, the kind you hear when a batter has just been hit by a pitch.

"It's been a long time since I visited this lovely old ball park, except to throw out an opening-day ball," continued the Mayor, "and even longer since I had talked to any true fans. But I've spoken with some today." The boos had now stopped. "I would like to announce that Judge Ford has just issued an order halting the bulldozers. And tomorrow I intend to go to the city council and ask them that they cancel plans—"

The roar of forty thousand fans drowned out the Mayor's voice.

For more than five minutes the cheers continued. Danny Wasocka turned toward the left-field bleachers. He could just barely make out the figures of Laura, Mama O'Leary, Tongue, Charmer, Scorecard Sam, and the rest of the Vipers. They were jumping up and down and pounding each other on the back.

"Looks like our friends are going to keep their old ball park," Danny said to Harrison.

"Yeah, man. Let's hope we're back here to play in it."

Coach Al Shinn was talking with Barrel Barnes. "What ever got into Pete Powers?"

"He must have gotten tired of winning batting titles while his team was losing," said Barrel.

"Maybe with Pete hustling and some of these fresh, new rookies there might be a pennant waving next year over Stratton Field."

"Last place to first? That only happens in bad baseball novels." Barrel smiled. "But you never know."

ABOUT THE AUTHOR

When Hal Higdon was growing up on the south side of Chicago, he and his friends used to play baseball in a vacant lot across the street from his apartment building. Written on a brick wall bordering that lot were the words in large white letters: STRATTON FIELD—HOME OF THE COBRAS.

He was never certain who gave his boyhood playing field that name or even the identity of that long-lost sandlot team. But when he decided to write a novel about a baseball team, its fans, and their efforts to save a beloved old ball park, he didn't have to search his memory long to find a name for that park and team.

Now a resident of Michigan City, Indiana, Mr. Higdon has written many magazine articles for *Sports Illustrated*, *National Geographic*, *True*, *TV Guide*, *Boys' Life*, and other publications. Two of his ten previous books also are novels for children. *The Horse That Played Center Field* features a boy named Kevin. *The Electronic Olympics* has a major character named Dave. And now *The Last Series* revolves around a girl named Laura. Those also happen to be the names of Hal Higdon's three children.